Teacher's Implementation Guide

BRITANNICA
Mathematics in Context

D1283368

HOLT, RINEHART AND WINSTON

Mathematics in Context is a comprehensive curriculum for the middle grades. It was developed in 1991 through 1997 in collaboration with the Wisconsin Center for Education Research, School of Education, University of Wisconsin-Madison and the Freudenthal Institute at the University of Utrecht, The Netherlands, with the support of the National Science Foundation Grant No. 9054928.

The revision of the curriculum was carried out in 2003 through 2005, with the support of the National Science Foundation Grant No. ESI 0137414.

National Science Foundation
Opinions expressed are those of the authors
and not necessarily those of the Foundation.

The Teacher Resource and Implementation Guide (TRIG) (1998) was written by Beth Cole, Thomas A. Romberg, Jan de Lange, and Sherian Foster.

The Teacher Implementation Guide (2006) is based on the TRIG (1998) and was written by Margaret R. Meyer with contributions from the staff of the Freudenthal Institute.

ISBN 0-03-040372-3

6 073 09 08 07

The *Mathematics in Context* Development Team

Development 1991–1997

Wisconsin Center for Education Research Staff

Thomas A. Romberg
Director

Joan Daniels Pedro
Assistant to the Director

Gail Burrill
Coordinator

Margaret R. Meyer
Coordinator

Project Staff

Jonathan Brendefur
Laura Brinker
James Browne
Jack Burrill
Rose Byrd
Peter Christiansen
Barbara Clarke
Doug Clarke
Beth R. Cole
Fae Dremock
Mary Ann Fix

Sherian Foster
James A, Middleton
Jasmina Milinkovic
Margaret A. Pligge
Mary C. Shafer
Julia A. Shew
Aaron N. Simon
Marvin Smith
Stephanie Z. Smith
Mary S. Spence

Freudenthal Institute Staff

Jan de Lange
Director

Els Feijs
Coordinator

Martin van Reeuwijk
Coordinator

Mieke Abels
Nina Boswinkel
Frans van Galen
Koeno Gravemeijer
Marja van den Heuvel-Panhuizen
Jan Auke de Jong
Vincent Jonker
Ronald Keijzer
Martin Kindt

Jansie Niehaus
Nanda Querelle
Anton Roodhardt
Leen Streefland
Adri Treffers
Monica Wijers
Astrid de Wild

Revision 2003–2005

Wisconsin Center for Education Research Staff

Thomas A. Romberg
Director

David C. Webb
Coordinator

Gail Burrill
Editorial Coordinator

Margaret A. Pligge
Editorial Coordinator

Freudenthal Institute Staff

Jan de Lange
Director

Truus Dekker
Coordinator

Mieke Abels
Content Coordinator

Monica Wijers
Content Coordinator

Project Staff

Sarah Ailts
Beth R. Cole
Erin Hazlett
Teri Hedges
Karen Hoiberg
Carrie Johnson
Jean Krusi
Elaine McGrath

Margaret R. Meyer
Anne Park
Bryna Rappaport
Kathleen A. Steele
Ana C. Stephens
Candace Ulmer
Jill Vettrus

Arthur Bakker
Peter Boon
Els Feijs
Dédé de Haan
Martin Kindt

Nathalie Kuijpers
Huub Nilwik
Sonia Palha
Nanda Querelle
Martin van Reeuwijk

Contents

Dear Mathematics Educator,

This book is designed for you! The *Teacher Implementation Guide* (TIG) provides a wealth of information for you to use as you look at *Mathematics in Context* (MiC) and also as you implement the curriculum.

Suggestions if you are looking at MiC for the first time:

- Read the overviews of the mathematical strand development on pages 6–22. They will give you insights into the mathematics in the complete program.

- Pacing for the year at each grade level and also specific details of the mathematical concepts for each unit begin on page 23. You may want to chose your specific level or look at the comprehensive listing.

- Assessment in MiC is very specialized; the design of the assessments and samples with scoring rubrics are found on pages 54–57. Consider especially the special learners in your classroom and the ability to assess cognitive learning levels.

- MiC is designed to enhance student learning. The philosophy of MiC and its history begin on page 58.

- The materials available for MiC and the layout of the materials in both Student Books and Teacher's Guides are detailed on pages. 62–68.

- Are you thinking of piloting MiC? Would you like to know how MiC will fit into your K-12 curriculum? See page 70 for information on pilots.

If you are a teacher or administrator preparing to implement MiC, you may find the following topics helpful:

- Implementation, Professional Development, Working with Families, Accessibility issues all are covered thoroughly on pages 71–83.

- Special suggestions for administrators are found on pages 83–85; this includes what to look for in an MiC classroom.

- Frequently Asked Questions may address any or all of your questions. See pages 86–90.

We have also included an alignment to the NCTM *Principles and Standards for School Mathematics* on pages 96–99.

We wish you success, and we hope that this book will make it easier for you to discover the benefits of Mathematics in Context!

The Mathematics in Context Development Team

RICH MATHEMATICS
REALISTIC CONTEXT
PROVEN RESULTS

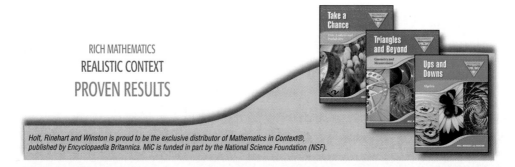

Holt, Rinehart and Winston is proud to be the exclusive distributor of Mathematics in Context®, published by Encyclopaedia Britannica. MiC is funded in part by the National Science Foundation (NSF).

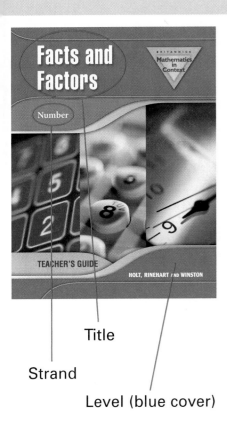

Title

Strand

Level (blue cover)

Curriculum Units

A full year's curriculum consists of 9 units. Units are available for three grade levels to make a total of 27 core units. The units are organized and color-coded by grade level. The color of the cover on both the Student Book and the Teacher's Guide indicates the level of that particular unit.

Red: Level 1

Blue: Level 2

Green: Level 3

Underneath the title for each unit is the strand designation

Each curriculum unit includes a non-consumable Student Book and a spiral bound Teacher's Guide.

LEVELS

STRANDS		1	2	3
	NUMBERS	Models You Can Count On Fraction Times More or Less	Facts and Factors Ratios and Rates	Revisiting Numbers
	ALGEBRA	Expressions and Formulas Comparing Quantities	Operations Building Formulas	Ups and Downs Graphing Equations Patterns and Figures Algebra Rules!
	GEOMETRY and MEASUREMENT	Figuring All the Angles Reallotment	Made to Measure Packages and Polygons Triangles and Beyond	It's All the Same Looking at an Angle
	DATA ANALYSIS and PROBABILITY	Picturing Numbers Take a Chance	Dealing with Data Second Chance	Insights into Data Great Predictions

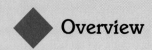
Program Description and Components

Program Description

Mathematics in Context (MiC) is a comprehensive middle school mathematics curriculum primarily used in grades 6–8. Development of the curriculum was funded in part by The National Science Foundation. The pedagogy and mathematical content of this program are consistent with the *Principles and Standards for School Mathematics* published by the National Council of Teachers of Mathematics (NCTM). MiC consists of 27 student units, 9 at each level. The units are organized by strand: Number, Geometry and Measurement, Algebra, and Data Analysis and Probability. Connections are a key feature of *Mathematics in Context*—connections among strands, connections to other disciplines, and connections between mathematics and meaningful problems in the real world. The rich mathematics in MiC is developed in a realistic context to engage students, motivate learning, and insure retention.

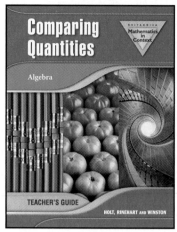

Level 1 Teacher's Guide

Program Components

- Student Editions   Nine individual paperback units at each level

    OR

    One hardbound text with all nine units for each level
- Teacher's Guides   Nine individual spiral-bound Teacher's Guides at each level

Level 2 Teacher's Guide

Program Resources

- Number Tools Teacher's Guide and Student Workbooks
- Algebra Tools Teacher's Guide and Student Workbooks
- Manipulatives Kit (One for all levels)
- Examview Test and Practice Generator
- Teaching Transparencies for each level
- Teacher Implementation Guide

Level 3 Teacher's Guide

Level 1 Student Book

Number Tools

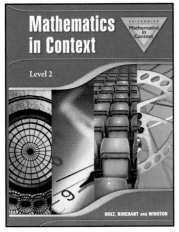

Level 2 Student Book

Algebra Tools

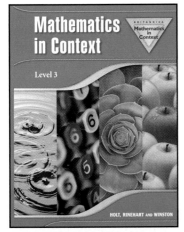

Level 3 Student Book

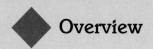

How MiC is Different

What Sets *Mathematics in Context* Apart from Other Middle Grades Math Curricula?

Mathematics in Context (MiC) builds on and connects to students' existing knowledge and skills:

As much as possible, MiC builds on students' existing mathematical knowledge. MiC tries to make students aware of mathematical phenomena in their surroundings. This helps students to connect math to the real world and increase their motivation to learn mathematics. MiC is designed to demonstrate that mathematics is relevant to students' daily lives and to make students aware of the mathematics that is part of their environment. In MiC, students are regularly asked to engage in problems in which they can use their informal notions and concepts, and recognize structures and patterns that exist around them.

MiC uses context in two ways—to develop mathematical concepts and ideas and to present areas of application of mathematical ideas and concepts:

The real world offers many contexts for the development of important mathematical concepts, ideas, and skills. These contexts also provide an anchor for students' thinking: a way for them to remember the concepts. Through decades of experimentation and experience at a practical level, the developers of MiC have gained insights into contexts that work for this purpose.

MiC uses models that support learning:

Students can make substantial progress in understanding basic ideas in mathematics if they are helped to develop "thinking models." In MiC, the number line, rectangular bar, and ratio table are powerful examples of such models. At first these might be used as *models of*, but later they serve as *models for*. For example, a rectangular bar can be used as a *model of* a submarine sandwich that is to be shared fairly. Later this same bar can be used as a visual *model for* the relationship of fractional parts or percents to a whole in any situation.

MiC emphasizes a variety of modes of representation including visualization:

In the past, little attention was given to using various modes of representation, even though it is well known that most students prefer to have visual representations rather than just text. This does not mean that student materials should simply include more photographs or illustrations. Rather, a wide range of meaningful representations are essential as seen in the use of text, sketches, tables, graphs, and formulas throughout the student materials in MiC.

The learning lines in MiC progress from informal to preformal to formal:

This principle of *progressive formalization* follows in part from the connection principle. Students often have informal notions from which more formal ideas can be built. MiC provides the opportunity for students to begin from their intuitive, informal knowledge and proceed carefully to a deeper, more formal conceptual understanding. It is important to recognize that students do not develop conceptual understanding in a matter of hours. Instead the long learning lines develop from the first unit to the last in order to assure that the learning objectives are met in ways that make sense to the students.

In MiC, the learning strands are intertwined and integrated:

The real phenomena in which mathematical structures and concepts are found usually contain mathematics from multiple strands. As a result, the four learning strands (Algebra, Number, Geometry/ Measurement, and Data Analysis/Probability) are intertwined rather than independent. The designers of MiC recognized that this approach benefits concept development and students' ability to recognize mathematical connections across strands.

MiC offers important mathematics:

A beginning point for the design of MiC was the belief that all students are able to do significant mathematics with understanding. When a challenging problem is posed, students have the opportunity to construct, design, or find different strategies to solve it. Some students will use more informal strategies, while others will use more formal approaches. Another principle of MiC is that it is always preferable for a student to use an informal strategy with understanding than it is to use a more formal strategy without understanding. In this way, more students have access to deeper mathematics.

MiC emphasizes basic skills, mathematizing, and reasoning in both lessons and assessments:

MiC recognizes that the goal of developing deeper mathematical conceptual understanding is supported by the goal of developing basic skills. These goals go hand in hand and are integrated in each of the units. This principle is also made explicit in the MiC Assessment Pyramid, which emphasizes a solid base of basic skills as a foundation for higher level reasoning goals.

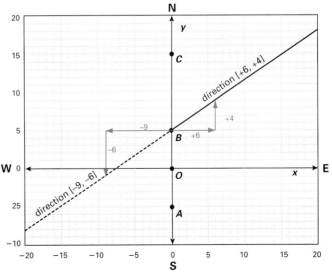

Number Strand: An Overview

Mathematical Content

The Number strand in *Mathematics in Context* emphasizes number sense, computations with number, and the ability to use number to better understand a situation. The broad category of number includes the concepts of magnitude, order, computation, relationships among numbers, and relationships among the various representations of number, such as fractions, decimals, and percents. In addition, ideas of ratio and proportion are developed gradually and are integrated with the other number representations. A theme that extends throughout the strand is using models as tools. Models are developed and used to help support student understanding of these concepts. The goals of the units within the Number strand are aligned with NCTM's *Principles and Standards for School Mathematics*.

Number Sense and Using Models as Tools

While the number sense theme is embedded in all the number units, this theme is emphasized in the additional resource, *Number Tools*. The activities in *Number Tools* reinforce students' understanding of ratios, fractions, decimals, and percents, and the connections between these representations. The using-models-as-tools theme is also embedded in every number unit.

Organization of the Number Strand

The Number strand has two major themes: develop and use models as tools and develop and use number sense. The units in the Number strand are organized into two main substrands: Rational Number and Number Theory. The map illustrates the strand organization.

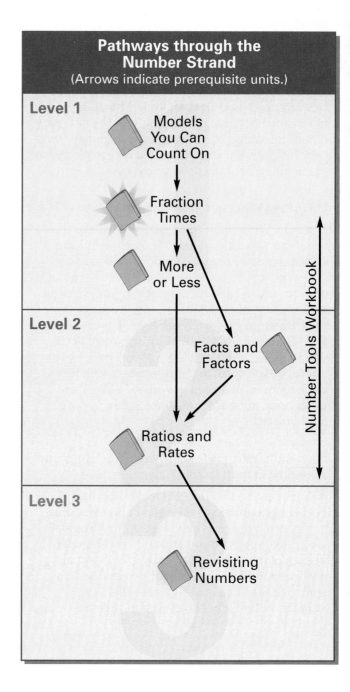

Pathways through the Number Strand
(Arrows indicate prerequisite units.)

Level 1 — Models You Can Count On → Fraction Times → More or Less

Level 2 — Facts and Factors → Ratios and Rates

Level 3 — Revisiting Numbers

Number Tools Workbook

The *Mathematics in Context* Approach to Number, Using Models as Tools

Throughout the Number strand, models are important problem-solving tools because they develop students' understanding of fractions, decimals, percents, and ratios to make connections.

 When a model is introduced, it is very closely related to a specific context; for example, in *Models You Can Count On*, students read gauges of a water tank and a coffee pot, and they solve problems related to a download bar.

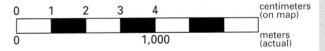

As students gain experience with the bar in different situations, it becomes more abstract and generalized and can be used as a tool to solve fraction and percent problems in general. The fraction bar as well as the percent bar give the students visual support.

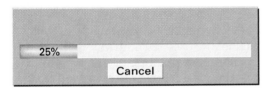

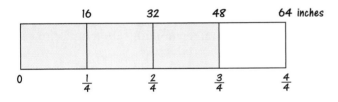

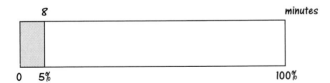

Double Number Line

Another model that students develop and use is the double number line. This model allows students to make accurate calculations and estimates as well, for all sorts of ratio problems, especially where real numbers are involved.

Pablo says, "That's almost 2 kg of apples."

Lia states, "That's about $1\frac{3}{4}$ kg of apples."

Pam suggests, "Use the scale as a double number line."

4. **a.** How will Pablo find the answer? What will Pablo estimate?

    b. How will Lia calculate the answer? What will she estimate?

    c. How will Pam use a double number line to estimate the cost of the apples?

The scale line on a map is also related to a double number line.

Number Line

The number line model is frequently used, and it is a general tool that applies to a wide range of problem contexts.

If students do not have a picture of a numbered number line, they can draw their own *empty number line* to make jumps by drawing curves between different lengths.

A number line is used to find the sum of two decimal numbers.

A jump of one and two jumps of 0.1 together make 1.2, so 1.6 + 1.2 = 2.8.

Note that on a single number line, fractions and decimals are seen as numbers—locations on number lines—and not as parts of wholes or operators.

Ratio Table

The difference between a ratio table and a double number line is that on a number line, the order of the numbers is fixed, whereas in a ratio table the numbers in the columns can be placed in any order that fits the calculation best.

Minutes	10	20	80	5	15	...
Miles	$\frac{1}{2}$	1	4	$\frac{1}{4}$	$\frac{3}{4}$	$4\frac{3}{4}$

When necessary, students can draw on their prior experience with specific and generalized models to make challenging problems more accessible. They are free to choose any model that they want to use to solve problems. Some students may prefer a bar model or a double number line because they give visual support, while other students may prefer a ratio table.

The *Mathematics in Context* Approach to Number, Number Sense

The Number strand gives students ample opportunity to develop computation, estimation, and number sense skills and to decide when to use each technique. In *Mathematics in Context*, it is more important for students to understand computation and use their own accurate computation strategies than it is for them to use formal algorithms that they don't understand. Because number concepts are an integral part of every unit in the curriculum—not just those in the Number strand—every unit extends students' understanding of number.

Rational Number

The first unit in the Number strand, *Models You Can Count On*, builds on students' informal knowledge of ratios, part-whole relationships, and benchmark percents. The unit emphasizes number models that can be used to support computation and develop students' number sense. For example, the ratio table is introduced with whole number ratios, and students develop strategies to generate equivalent ratios in the table.

These strategies are made explicit: adding, times 10, doubling, subtracting, multiplying, halving. Students informally add, multiply, and divide benchmark fractions. The context of money and the number line offer the opportunity to reinforce computations with decimal numbers.

The second unit in the Number strand, *Fraction Times*, makes connections and builds on the models, skills, and concepts that are developed in the unit *Models You Can Count On*.

Fraction Times further develops and extends students' understanding of relationships among fractions, decimals, and percents. Bar models and pie charts are used to make connections between fractions and percents. Bars or ratio tables are used to compare, informally add and subtract, and simplify fractions. The context of money is chosen to multiply whole numbers with decimals and to change fractions into decimals and decimals into fractions. When students calculate a fraction of a fraction by using fractions of whole numbers, students informally multiply fractions. Some of the operations with fractions are formalized.

In *More or Less*, students formalize, connect, and expand their knowledge of fractions, decimals, and percents in number and geometry contexts. Problems involving the multiplication of decimals and percents are introduced. Students use benchmark fractions to find percents and discounts. They use one-step multiplication calculations to compute sale price and prices that include tax. They also use percents in a geometric context to find the dimensions of enlarged or reduced photocopies and then connect the percent increase to multiplication.

The unit *Facts and Factors* revisits the operations with fractions that were not formalized in the unit *Fraction Times*. This unit is a unit in the Number Theory substrand. The area model is developed and used to increase students' understanding of how to multiply fractions and mixed numbers.

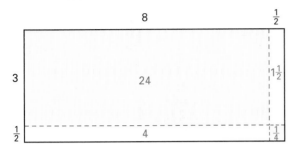

While *More or Less* extends students' understanding of the connections between fractions and decimals, the unit *Ratios and Rates* focuses on the connections between these types of rational numbers and per-cents. It relates ratios to fractions, decimals, and percents and introduces students to ratio as a single number. The use of number tools from earlier units is revisited. The double number line is revisited in the context of scale lines on a map. The ratio table is another model that is used in the context of scale. *Ratios and Rates* extends students' understanding of ratio. The use of ratio tables helps students under-stand that ratios and rates are also averages. When students start to compare ratios, the terms *relative comparison* and *absolute comparison* are introduced, and students discover the value of comparing ratios as opposed to looking only at absolute amounts. In realistic situations, students investigate part-part ratios and part-whole ratios.

The final unit of the Number strand, *Revisiting Numbers*, integrates concepts from both substrands. Rational number ideas are reviewed, extended, and formalized. This unit builds on experiences with the unit *Ratios and Rates* to further explore rates. In the context of speed, students use ratio tables to calculate rates and change units. Students solve context problems where operations (multiplication and division) with fractions and mixed numbers are involved. They use these experiences to solve "bare" problems by thinking of a context that fits the bare problem. Supported by the context and the models they can count on (a double number line, a ratio table, and the area model), students develop their own strategies to solve all types of problems.

Number Theory

The Level 2 number unit, *Facts and Factors*, helps students to get a better understanding of the base-ten number system. Students study number notation, the naming of large numbers, powers of ten, powers of two, and exponential notation. Students investigate how a calculator shows very large numbers and make connections with the product of a number and a power of ten: the scientific notation.

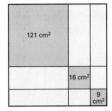

They use scientific notation only in a "passive" way. Very small numbers are investigated in the number unit *Revisiting Numbers*. Students use several strategies, including upside-down arithmetic trees, to factor composite numbers into their prime factors. Using the sides and area of a square of graph paper, the relationship between squares and square roots is explored. This unit expands students' understanding of rational and irrational numbers at an informal level.

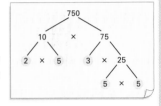

The unit *Revisiting Numbers* is the last unit in the Number strand. A conceptual understanding of natural numbers, whole numbers, integers, rational numbers, irrational numbers, and real numbers is developed. This unit builds on students' previous experience with numbers.

Investigations of relationships between operations and their inverses promote understanding of whole numbers, integers, and rational and irrational numbers. The calculator notation and the scientific notation for large numbers are reviewed from the unit *Facts and Factors* and extended with these notations for small numbers. Multiplication and division with positive and negative powers of ten are formalized. Supported by contexts and the area model, the commutative property, the distributive property, and the associative property are investi-gated and formalized.

Algebra Strand: An Overview

Mathematical Content

The Algebra strand in *Mathematics in Context* emphasizes algebra as a language used to study relationships among quantities. Students learn to describe these relationships with a variety of representations and to make connections among these representations. The goal is for students to understand the use of algebra as a tool to solve problems that arise in the real world or in the world of mathematics, where symbolic representations can be temporarily freed of meaning to bring a deeper understanding of the problem. Students move from preformal to formal strategies to solve problems, learning to make reasonable choices about which algebraic representation, if any, to use. The goals of the units within the Algebra strand are aligned with NCTM's *Principles and Standards for School Mathematics*.

Algebra Tools and Other Resources

The *Algebra Tools* Workbook provides materials for additional practice and further exploration of algebraic concepts that can be used in conjunction with units in the Algebra strand or independently from individual units. The use of a graphing calculator is optional in the Student Books. The Teacher's Guides provide additional questions if graphing calculators are used.

Organization of the Algebra Strand

The theme of change and relationships encompasses every unit in the Algebra strand. The strand is organized into three substrands: Patterns and Regularities, Restrictions, and Graphing. Note that units within a substrand are also connected to units in other substrands.

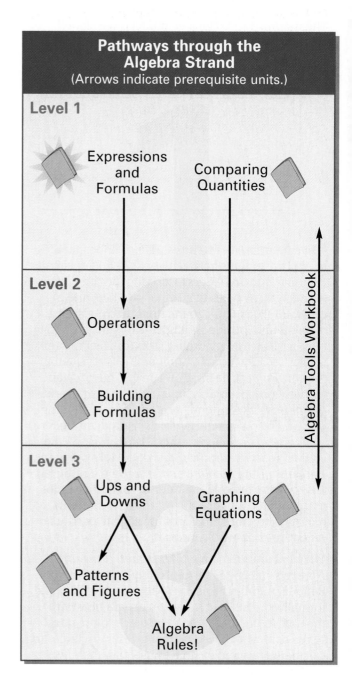

Pathways through the Algebra Strand
(Arrows indicate prerequisite units.)

Level 1 — Expressions and Formulas, Comparing Quantities

Level 2 — Operations, Building Formulas

Level 3 — Ups and Downs, Graphing Equations, Patterns and Figures, Algebra Rules!

Algebra Tools Workbook

Patterns and Regularities

In the Patterns and Regularities substrand, students explore and represent patterns to develop an understanding of formulas, equations, and expressions. The first unit, *Expressions and Formulas*, uses arrow language and arithmetic trees to represent situations. With these tools, students create and use word formulas that are the precursors to algebraic equations. The problem below shows how students use arrow language to write and solve equations with a single unknown.

The students use an arrow string to find the height of a stack of cups.

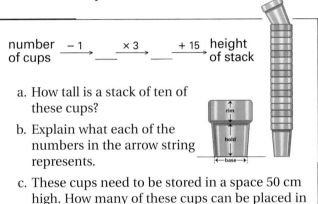

a. How tall is a stack of ten of these cups?

b. Explain what each of the numbers in the arrow string represents.

c. These cups need to be stored in a space 50 cm high. How many of these cups can be placed in a stack? Explain how you found your answer.

As problems and calculations become more complicated, students adapt arrow language to include multiplication and division. When dealing with all four arithmetic operations, students learn about the order of operations and use another new tool—arithmetic trees—to help them organize their work and prioritize their calculations. Finally, students begin to generalize their calculations for specific problems using word formulas.

saddle height (in cm) = inseam (in cm) × 1.08
frame height (in cm) = inseam (in cm) × 0.66 + 2

In *Building Formulas*, students explore direct and recursive formulas (formulas in which the current term is used to calculate the next term) to describe patterns. By looking at the repetition of a basic pattern, students are informally introduced to the distributive property. In *Patterns and Figures*, students continue to use and formalize the ideas of direct and recursive formulas and work formally with algebraic expressions, such as $2(n + 1)$.

In a recursive (or NEXT-CURRENT) formula, the next number or term in a sequence is found by performing an operation on the current term according to a formula. For many of the sequences in this unit, the next term is a result of adding or subtracting a fixed number from the current term of the sequence. Operations with linear expressions are connected to "Number Strips," or arithmetic sequences.

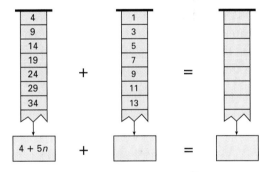

Students learn that they can combine sequences by addition and subtraction. In *Patterns and Figures*, students also encounter or revisit other mathematical topics such as rectangular and triangular numbers. This unit broadens their mathematical experience and makes connections between algebra and geometry.

In the unit *Graphing Equations*, linear equations are solved in an informal and preformal way. The last unit, *Algebra Rules!*, integrates and formalizes the content of algebra substrands. In this unit, a variety of methods to solve linear equations is used in a formal way. Connections to other strands are also formalized. For example, area models of algebraic expressions are used to highlight relationships between symbolic representations and the Geometry and Measurement strands. In *Algebra Rules!*, students also work with quadratic expressions.

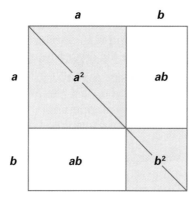

The Patterns and Regularities substrand includes a unit that is closely connected to the Number strand, *Operations*. In this unit, students build on their informal understanding of positive and negative numbers and use these numbers in addition, subtraction, and multiplication. Division of negative numbers is addressed in *Revisiting Numbers* and in *Algebra Rules!*

Restrictions

In the Restrictions substrand, the range of possible solutions to the problems is restricted because the mathematical descriptions of the problem contexts require at least two equations. In *Comparing Quantities*, students explore informal methods for solving systems of equations through nonroutine, yet realistic, problem situations such as running a school store, renting canoes, and ordering in a restaurant.

Within such contexts as bartering, students are introduced to the concept of substitution (exchange) and are encouraged to use symbols to represent problem scenarios. Adding and subtracting relationships graphically and multiplying the values of a graph by a number help students develop a sense of operations with expressions.

To solve problems about the combined costs of varying quantities of items such as pencils and erasers, students use charts to identify possible combinations. They also identify and use the number patterns in these charts to solve problems.

**Costs of Combinations
(in dollars)**

5					
4					
3					
2	80				
1		76			
0					

Number of Umbrellas (vertical axis), Number of Caps (horizontal axis: 0 1 2 3 4 5)

Students' work with problems involving combinations of items is extended as they explore problems about shopping. Given two "picture equations" of different quantities of two items and their combined price, students find the price of a single item. Next, they informally solve problems involving three equations and three variables within the context of a restaurant and the food ordered by people at different tables.

This context also informally introduces matrices. At the end of the unit, students revisit these problem scenarios more formally as they use variables and formal equations to represent and solve problems.

ORDER	TACO	SALAD	DRINK	TOTAL
1	2	4	—	⊄10
2	1	2	3	⊄8
3	3	—	3	⊄9
4	1	2	—	
5	1	—	1	
6	2	2	1	
7	4	2	3	
8				
9				
10				

In *Graphing Equations*, students move from locating points using compass directions and bearings to using graphs and algebraic manipulation to find the point of intersection of two lines.

Students may use graphing calculators to support their work as they move from studying slope to using slope to write equations for lines. Visualizing frogs jumping toward or away from a path helps students develop formal algebraic methods for solving a system of linear equations. In *Algebra Rules!*, the relationship between the point of intersection of two lines (A and B) and the *x*-intercept of the difference between those two lines (A – B) is explored. Students also find that parallel lines relate to a system of equations that have no solution.

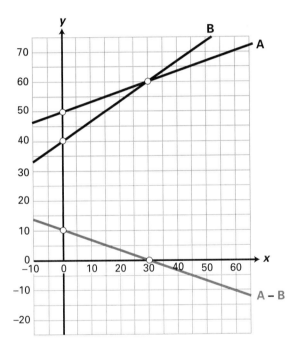

Graphing

The Graphing substrand, which builds on students' experience with graphs in previous number and statistics units, begins with *Expressions and Formulas* where students relate formulas to graphs and read information from a graph.

Operations, which is in the Patterns and Regularities substrand, is also related to the Graphing substrand since it formally introduces the coordinate system.

In *Ups and Downs*, students use equations and graphs to investigate properties of graphs corresponding to a variety of relationships: linear, quadratic, and exponential growth as well as graphs that are periodic.

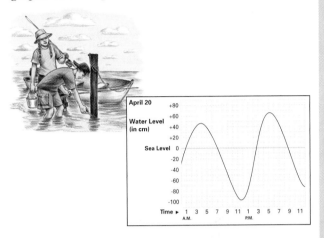

In *Graphing Equations*, students explore the equation of a line in slope and *y*-intercept form. They continuously formalize their knowledge and adopt conventional formal vocabulary and notation, such as origin, quadrant, and *x*-axis, as well as the ordered pairs notation (*x, y*). In this unit, students use the slope-intercept form of the equation of a line, $y = mx + b$. Students may use graphing calculators to support their work as they move from studying slope to using slope to write equations for lines. Students should now be able to recognize linearity from a graph, a table, and a formula and know the connections between those representations. In the last unit in the Algebra strand, *Algebra Rules!*, these concepts are formalized and the *x*-intercept is introduced. Adding and subtracting relationships graphically and multiplying the values of a graph by a number help students develop a sense of operations with expressions.

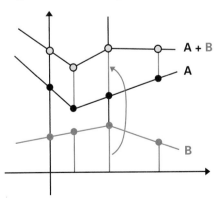

Geometry and Measurement Strand: An Overview

In the MiC units, measurement concepts and skills are not treated as a separate strand. Many measurement topics are closely related to what students learn in geometry. The geometry and measurement units contain topics such as similarity, congruency, perimeter, area, and volume. The identification of and application with a variety of shapes, both two-dimensional and three dimensional, is also addressed.

The developmental principles behind geometry in *Mathematics in Context* are drawn from Hans Freudenthal's idea of "grasping space." Throughout the strand, ideas of geometry and measurement are explored. Geometry includes movement and space—not just the study of shapes. The major goals for this strand are to develop students' ability to describe what is seen from different perspectives and to use principles of orientation and navigation to find their way from one place to another.

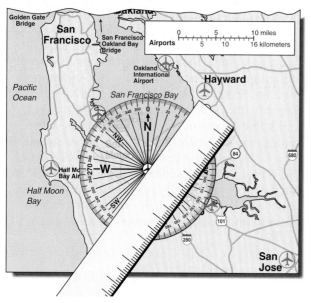

The emphasis on spatial sense is related to how most people actually use geometry. The development of students' spatial sense allows them to solve problems in the real world, such as identifying a car's blind spots, figuring out how much material to buy for a project, deciding whether a roof or ramp is too steep, and finding the height or length of something that cannot be measured directly, such as a tree or a building.

Mathematical Content

In *Mathematics in Context*, geometry is firmly anchored in the physical world. The problem contexts involve space and action, and students represent these physical relationships mathematically.

Throughout the curriculum, students discover relationships between shapes and develop the ability to explain and use geometry in the real world. By the end of the curriculum, students work more formally with geometric concepts such as parallelism, congruence, and similarity, and use traditional methods of notation as well.

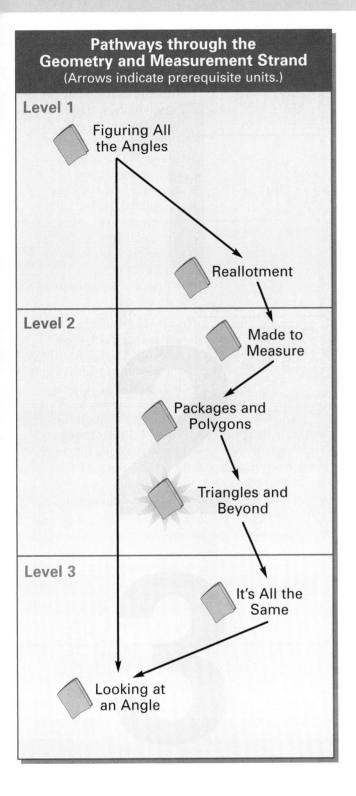

Pathways through the Geometry and Measurement Strand
(Arrows indicate prerequisite units.)

Level 1

Figuring All the Angles

Reallotment

Level 2

Made to Measure

Packages and Polygons

Triangles and Beyond

Level 3

It's All the Same

Looking at an Angle

Organization of the Geometry and Measurement Strand

Visualization and representation is a pervasive theme in the Geometry strand and is developed in all of the Geometry and Measurement strand units. The units are organized into two substrands: Orientation and Navigation, and Shape and Construction. The development of measurement skills and concepts overlaps these two substrands and is also integrated throughout other *Mathematics in Context* units in Number, Algebra, and Data Analysis.

Orientation and Navigation

The Orientation and Navigation substrand is introduced in *Figuring All the Angles*, in which students are introduced to the cardinal, or compass, directions and deal with the problems that arise when people in different positions describe a location with directions. Students use maps and compass headings to identify the positions of airplanes. They look at angles as turns, or changes in direction, as well as the track made by a sled in the snow. They discern different types of angles and learn formal notations and terms: vertex, $\angle A$, and so on. The rule for the sum of the angles in a triangle is informally introduced. To find angle measurements students use instruments such as a protractor and compass card.

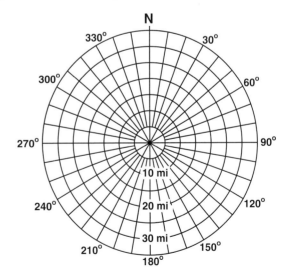

In *Looking at an Angle*, the last unit in the Geometry strand, the tangent ratio is informally introduced. The steepness of a vision line, the sun's rays, a ladder, and the flight path of a hang glider can all be modeled by a right triangle. Considering the glide ratio of hang gliders leads to formalization of the tangent ratio. Two other ratios between the sides of a right triangle are introduced, the sine and the cosine. This leads to formalization of the use of the Pythagorean theorem and its converse.

Shape and Construction

Reallotment is the first unit in the Shape and Construction substrand. Students measure and calculate the perimeters and areas of quadrilaterals, circles, triangles, and irregular polygons. Students learn and use relations between units of measurement within the Customary system and the Metric System.

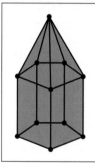

Does Euler's formula work for a five-sided tower? Explain your answer

Solids are introduced in *Packages and Polygons*. Students compare polyhedra with their respective nets, use bar models to understand the concept of rigidity, and use Euler's formula to formally investigate the relationships among the numbers of faces, vertices, and edges of polyhedra.

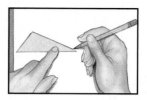

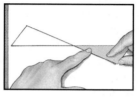

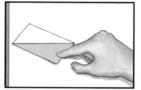

In *Triangles and Beyond*, students develop a more formal understanding of the properties of triangles, which they use to construct triangles. The concepts of parallel lines, congruence, and transformation are introduced, and students investigate the properties of parallel lines and parallelograms. A preformal introduction to the Pythagorean theorem is presented.

After studying this unit, students should be able to recognize and classify triangles and quadrilaterals. In the unit *It's All the Same*, students develop an understanding of congruency, similarity, and the properties of similar triangles and then use these ideas to solve problems. Their work with similarity and parallelism leads them to make generalizations about the angles formed when a transversal intersects parallel lines, and the Pythagorean theorem is formalized.

If a triangle has a right angle, then the square on the longest side has the same area as the other two combined.

Measurement

The concept of a measurement system, standard-ized units, and their application overlaps the sub-strands of Orientation and Navigation, and Shape and Construction. Furthermore, the development and application of measurement skills is integrated throughout units in the Number, Algebra, and Data Analysis strands, through topics such as use of ratio and proportion, finding and applying scale factors, and solving problems involving rates (for instance, distance-velocity-time relationships).

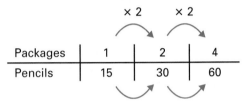

	×2		×2	
Packages	1		2	4
Pencils	15		30	60

In *Mathematics in Context*, the Metric System is used not only as a measurement system, but also as a model to promote understanding of decimal numbers.

The unit *Made to Measure* is a thematic measure-ment unit where students work with standard and non-standard units to understand the systems and processes of measurement. They begin by studying historic units of measure such as foot, pace, and fathom (the length of outstretched arms). Students use their own measurements in activities about length, area, volume, and angle and then examine why standardized units are necessary for each.

The relationships between measurement units are embedded in the number unit *Models You Can Count On*, where students explore conversions between measures of length within the Metric System. The measurement of area in both Metric and Customary Systems is explicitly addressed in the unit *Reallotment*. Students also learn some simple relationships between metric and customary measurement units, such as 1 kilogram is about 2.2 pounds, and other general conversion rules to support estimations across different measurement systems. In *Reallotment*, *Made to Measure*, and *Packages and Polygons*, the concepts of volume and surface area are developed. Strategies that were applied to find area measurements in *Reallotment* are used to derive formulas for finding the volume of a cylinder, pyramid, and cone.

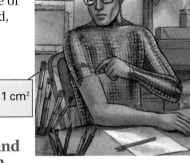

1 cm²

Visualization and Representation

Visualization and representation is a component of every geometry unit. In *Mathematics in Context*, this theme refers to exploring figures from different perspectives and then communicating about their appearance or characteristics.

In *Reallotment*, students use visualizations and representations to find the areas of geometric figures. They decide how to reshape geometric figures and group smaller units into larger, easy-to-count units. They also visualize and represent the results for changing the dimensions of a solid. In the unit *It's All the Same*, students visualize triangles to solve problems.

The Data Analysis and Probability Strand: An Overview

One thing is for sure: our lives are full of uncertainty. We are not certain what the weather will be tomorrow or which team will win a game or how accurate a pulse rate really is. Data analysis and probability are ways to help us measure variability and uncertainty. A central feature of both data analysis and probability is that these disciplines help us make numerical conjectures about important questions.

The techniques and tools of data analysis and probability allow us to understand general patterns for a set of outcomes from a given situation such as tossing a coin, but it is important to remember that a given outcome is only part of the larger pattern. Many students initially tend to think of individual cases and events, but gradually they learn to think of all features of data sets and of probabilities as proportions in the long run.

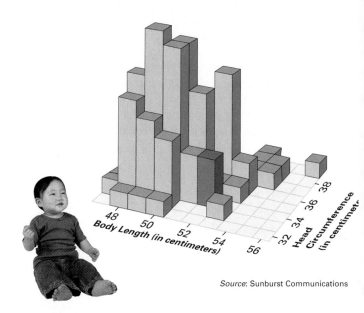

Source: Sunburst Communications

The MiC Approach to Data Analysis and Probability

The Data Analysis and Probability units in MiC emphasize dealing with data, developing an understanding of chance and probability, using probability in situations connected to data analysis, and developing critical thinking skills.

The strand begins with students' intuitive understanding of the data analysis concepts of *most, least,* and *middle* in relation to different types of *graphical representations* that show *the distribution of data* and the probability concepts of *fairness* and *chance.* As students gradually formalize these ideas, they use a variety of counting strategies and graphical representations. In the culminating units of this strand, they use formal rules and strategies for calculating probabilities and finding measures of central tendency and spread.

Throughout this development, there is a constant emphasis on interpreting conclusions made by students and suggested in the media or other sources. In order for students to make informed decisions, they must understand how information is collected, represented, and summarized, and they examine conjectures made from the information based on this understanding. They learn about all phases of an investigative cycle, starting with questions, collecting data, analyzing them, and communicating about the conclusions. They are introduced to inference-by-sampling to collect data and reflect on possible sources of bias. They develop notions of random sampling, variation and central tendency, correlation, and regression. Students create, interpret, and reflect on a wide range of graphical representations of data and relate these representations to numerical summaries such as mean, mode, and range.

Organization of the Strand

Statistical reasoning based on data is addressed in all Data Analysis and Probability units. Students' work in these units is organized into two substrands: Data Analysis and Chance. As illustrated in the following map of the strand, the three core units that focus on data analysis are *Picturing Numbers*, *Dealing with Data*, and *Insights into Data*. The two units that focus on probability are *Take a Chance* and *Second Chance*. The sixth core unit in this strand, *Great Predictions*, integrates data analysis and probability.

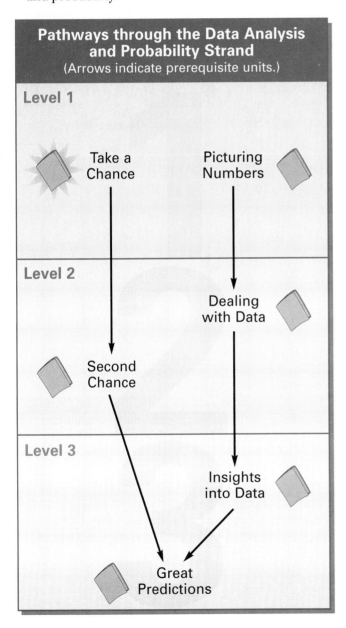

Pathways through the Data Analysis and Probability Strand
(Arrows indicate prerequisite units.)

Level 1

Take a Chance

Picturing Numbers

Level 2

Dealing with Data

Second Chance

Level 3

Insights into Data

Great Predictions

Data Analysis

In the units of the Data Analysis substrand, students collect, depict, describe, and analyze data. Using the statistical tools they develop, they make inferences and draw conclusions based on data sets.

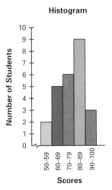

Number of Babies in Litter

The substrand begins with *Picturing Numbers*. Students collect data and display them in tabular and graphical forms, such as histograms, number line plots, and pie charts. Measures of central tendency, such as the mean, are used informally as students interpret data and make conjectures.

In *Dealing with Data*, students create and interpret scatter plots, box plots, and stem-and-leaf plots, in addition to other graphical representations. The mean, median, mode, range, and quartiles are used to summarize data sets. Students investigate data sets with outliers and make conclusions about the appropriate use of the mean and median.

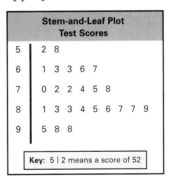

Stem-and-Leaf Plot
Test Scores

5	2 8
6	1 3 3 6 7
7	0 2 2 4 5 8
8	1 3 3 4 5 6 7 7 9
9	5 8 8

Key: 5 | 2 means a score of 52

Sampling is addressed across this substrand, but in particular in *Insights into Data*, starting with informal notions of representative samples, randomness, and bias. Students gather data using various sampling techniques and investigate the differences between a survey and a sample. They create a simulation to answer questions about a situation. Students also consider how graphical information can be misleading, and they are introduced informally to the concepts of regression and correlation.

In *Great Predictions*, students learn to recognize the variability in random samples and deepen their understanding of the key statistical concepts of randomness, sample size, and bias. As the capstone unit to the Data Analysis and Probability strand, data and chance concepts and techniques are integrated and used to inform conclusions about data.

Chance

Beginning with the concept of fairness, *Take a Chance* progresses to everyday situations involving chance. Students use coins and number cubes to conduct repeated trials of an experiment. A chance ladder is used as a model throughout the unit to represent the range from impossible to certain and to ground the measure of chance as a number between 0 and 1. Students also use tree diagrams to organize and count, and they use benchmark fractions, ratios, and percents to describe the probability of various outcomes and combinations.

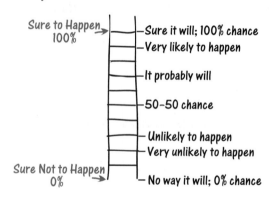

The second probability unit, *Second Chance*, further develops students' understanding of fairness and the quantification of chance. Students make chance statements from data presented in two-way tables and in graphs.

	Men	Women	Total
Glasses	32	3	35
No Glasses	56	39	95
Total	88	42	130

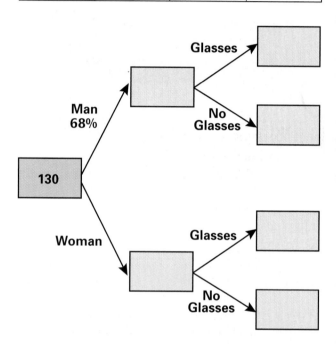

Students also reason about theoretical probability and use chance trees as well as an area model to compute chances for compound events. They use information from surveys, experiments, and simulations to investigate experimental probability. Students also explore probability concepts such as complementary events and dependent and independent events.

These concepts are elaborated further in the final unit of the strand, *Great Predictions*. This last unit develops the concepts of expected value, features of independent and dependent events, and the role of chance in world events.

Critical Reasoning

Critical reasoning about data and chance is a theme that exists in every unit of the Data Analysis and Probability strand. In *Picturing Numbers*, students informally consider factors that influence data collection, such as the wording of questions on a survey, and they compare different graphs of the same data set. They also use statistical data to build arguments for or against environmental policies.

In *Take a Chance*, students use their informal knowledge of fairness and equal chances as they evaluate decision-making strategies.

In *Dealing with Data*, students explore how the graphical representation of a data set influences the conjectures and conclusions that are suggested by the data. They compare advantages and disadvantages of various graphs and explore what you learn from using different measures of central tendency.

Throughout the curriculum, students are asked to view representations critically. Developing a critical attitude is especially promoted in *Insights into Data*, when students analyze graphs from mass media.

In *Second Chance*, students explore the notion of dependency (for instance, the relation of gender and wearing glasses) and analyze statements about probabilities (for instance, about guessing during a test).

In *Great Predictions*, students study unusual samples to decide whether they occurred by chance or for some other reason (pollution, for instance). They explore how expected values and probability can help them make decisions and when this information could be misleading.

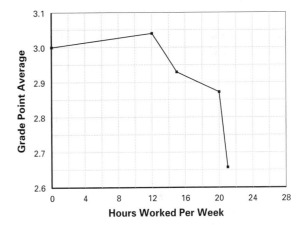

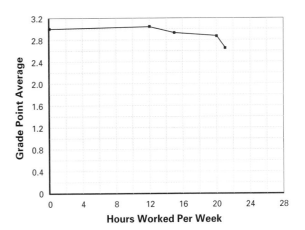

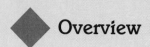

Curriculum Map

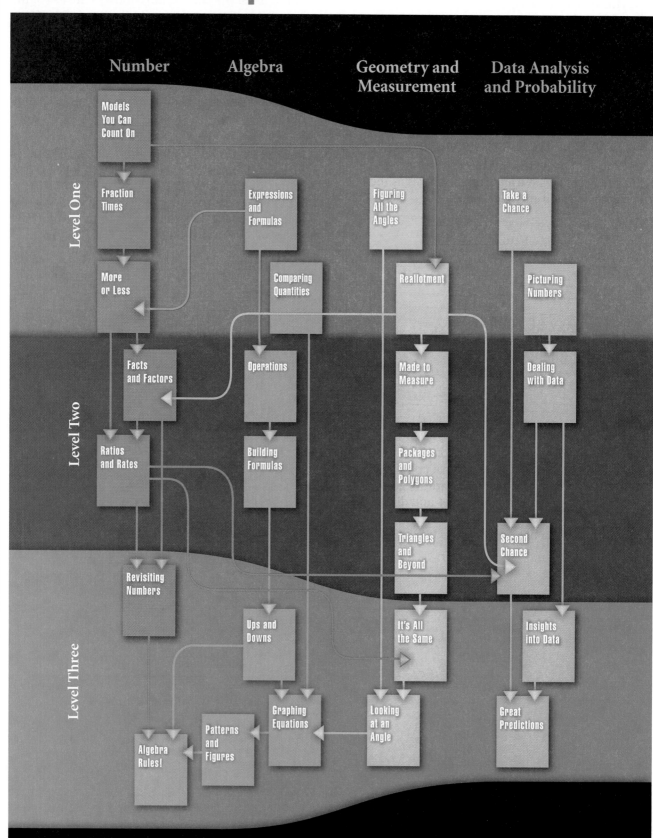

	Number	Algebra	Geometry and Measurement	Data Analysis and Probability
Level One	Models You Can Count On			
	Fraction Times	Expressions and Formulas	Figuring All the Angles	Take a Chance
	More or Less	Comparing Quantities	Reallotment	Picturing Numbers
Level Two	Facts and Factors	Operations	Made to Measure	Dealing with Data
	Ratios and Rates	Building Formulas	Packages and Polygons	
			Triangles and Beyond	Second Chance
Level Three	Revisiting Numbers			
		Ups and Downs	It's All the Same	Insights into Data
		Graphing Equations	Looking at an Angle	Great Predictions
	Algebra Rules!	Patterns and Figures		

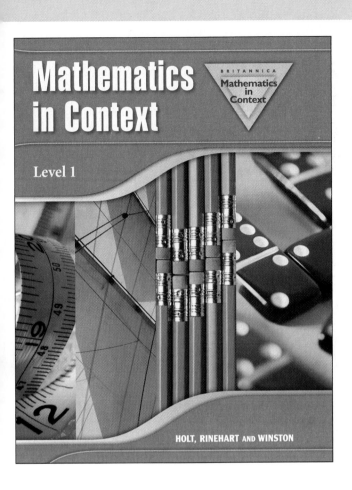

Level 1: Order of Implementation and Pacing Guide

Picturing Numbers	**14 days**
Mean, median, and mode; displaying and interpreting data	
Models You Can Count On	**21 days**
Models for comparing and computing with fractions, decimals, percents, and ratios	
Expressions and Formulas	**16 days**
Inverse operations; order of operations; application of formulas	
Take a Chance	**14 days**
Independent events; counting strategies; multiple representations of simple probabilities	
Fraction Times	**16 days**
Operations with fractions; ordering fractions	
Figuring All the Angles	**15 days**
Angle measure; rectangular grids; direction	
Comparing Quantities	**15 days**
Patterns that lead to informal solutions of systems of equations; concept of variable	
Reallotment	**18 days**
Perimeter, areas, surface area, and volume	
More or Less	**14 days**
Ratios; multiplication of decimals	
Total days for teaching these units	**139 days**

Picturing Numbers

Students use various kinds of graphs to represent and interpret data.

The use of bar graphs is reviewed and formalized. Emphasis is placed on labeling the axes and providing a title.

A variety of representations of graphs is used to "tell the story" behind the collected data. Students conduct surveys about such things as their future profession or favorite television programs and present the results using pictographs, number line plots, stacked bar graphs, and circle graphs (pie charts).

They consider questions such as: Can two graphs represent the same data? What kind of question can best be answered using a bar graph? What kind of question can best be answered with a pie graph of the same data?

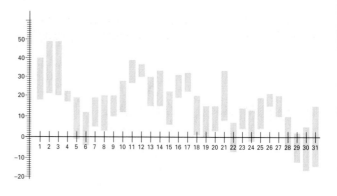

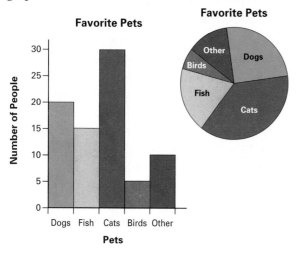

Students use graphs to answer questions about measures of central tendency, such as mean or mode. Use of formal terms and algorithms is not emphasized; understanding the concept is far more important at this point.

Then line graphs or plot-over-time graphs are introduced using daily temperatures. Students use terms like *maximum, minimum,* and *range* to describe the distribution of data.

When students have finished this unit, they will:

- create and interpret different kinds of graphs: bar graphs, pie graphs, pictographs, stacked bar graphs, line graphs, and number line plots;
  - Students are introduced to these types of graphs. These will be revisited in the units *Dealing with Data* and *Insights into Data*.
- collect data and represent them in tabular and graphic form;
  - Students can use their own survey results to create tables and graphs representing the data they collected.
  - They can identify advantages and disadvantages of different graphical representations.
- describe data numerically using mean, median, mode, range, maximum, and minimum; and
  - Students know different ways to find the mean from a given data set.
  - They can describe the other numbers of center in their own words; a more formal review takes place in later units.
- use data, graphs, and numeric characteristics to build arguments and compare data sets.
  - Students can describe patterns and other features of datasets in graphs and other diagrams.

Models You Can Count On

The focus of this unit, is to introduce and develop several number models that students can use as tools to solve problems.

Ratio Table

Number of Boxes	20	10	5
Price (in dollars)	240	120	60

Bar Model

Double Number Line

Number Line

A jump of 1 and two jumps of 0.1 make together 1.2, so 2.8 − 1.6 = 1.2

When students have finished this unit, they will:

- develop and use models;
  - Students develop strategies to generate new numbers in a ratio table (equivalent ratios);
  - They use a ratio table as an organizational tool.
  - They develop a conceptual understanding of ratio.
  - They represent and make sense of calculations involving fractions and percents using a bar model (percent bar).
  - They represent and make sense of calculations involving fractions and decimals using a double number line.
  - They informally multiply and divide fractions using a double number line.
  - They use scale lines and maps to determine distance and use double number lines to relate travel time and distance.
- develop number sense and a conceptual understanding of fractions, decimals, percents, and ratios.
  - Students revise whole number operations (in a ratio table).
  - They order and compare fractions and decimals on a single number line.
  - They understand that a fraction is the result of a division and a description of a part-whole relationship.
  - They use fractions as numbers and as measures.
  - They connect benchmark percents (1%, 10%, 25%, 33%, and 50%) to fractions.
  - They understand 100% as a whole.
  - They combine benchmark percents to find non-benchmark percents, for example, using 10% and 5% to find 15%.
  - They use benchmark percents to find a part, given a percent and a whole.
  - They use benchmark percents to find a percent, given a part and a whole.
  - They choose their own model to solve problems where ratios and proportions, fractions, decimals, and percents are involved.

Expressions and Formulas

In this unit, students make change and determine grocery bills that involve produce, meat, or cheese, sold by the pound. They also find prices in non-grocery contexts such as calculating a plumber's bill. To keep track of the complicated sequences of calculations necessary to do these problems, students are introduced to several new tools.

Arrow strings are introduced to organize computations. In this example, an arrow string is used to show the change for a $3.70 purchase, named the *small-coins-and-bills-first method*:

$$\$3.70 \xrightarrow{+\,\$0.05} \$3.75 \xrightarrow{+\,\$0.25} \$4.00$$
$$\xrightarrow{+\,\$1.00} \$5.00 \xrightarrow{+\,\$5.00} \$10.00 \xrightarrow{+\,\$10.00}$$
$$\$20.00$$

Later in the unit, the arrow strings are also used to consider the order of operations, reverse operations, and as a means to represent (word) formulas.

Conversion rules from miles to kilometers, and vice versa, are also used.

Students use arithmetic trees to study the order of operations. They begin to generalize their calculations for specific problems using word formulas. Reading a graph representing a linear relationship is introduced.

When students have finished this unit, they will:

- describe and perform a series of calculations using arrow strings and arithmetic trees;
  - Students will also be familiar with the process of making change.

- use conventional rules and grouping symbols to perform a sequence of calculations and apply the order of operations;
- use and interpret simple formulas;
  - For example, students will apply rules to convert from miles to kilometers, and vice versa.
  - The concept of equivalent formulas, or equations, is also introduced.
- use reverse operations to find the input for a given output;
- rewrite numerical expressions to facilitate calculation;
  - Students informally use the associative and commutative properties of addition to simplify a string of computations.
- interpret relationships displayed in formulas, tables, and graphs;
- use word variables to describe a formula or procedure;
- begin generalizing from patterns to symbolic relationships;
- solve problems using the relationship between a mathematical procedure and its inverse; and
- use various representations, for example, arrow language, arithmetic tree, words, to describe patterns and formulas and to solve problems.

Take a Chance

Many of the problems in this unit, are set in the context of the daily life of two fictional students, Hillary and Robert. These students consider how and whether such tools as number cubes, spinners, or coins can be used in a particular situation to make a fair decision.

A numerical value for the probability that an event occurs is introduced using a scale known as a *chance ladder.* Students order different events on this scale according to the probability each event will occur. They select a point on the scale to represent the chance of an event.

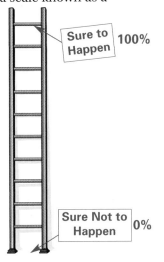

At first, chances are only estimated. Most questions focus on "Is this fair?" "How many possible outcomes exist?" "How many of these are favorable?" "Which is the more likely outcome?" Later in the unit, students calculate chances and express them as ratios, fractions, or percents. This is done for experimental chances (for example, results of tossing an item 30 times), and for theoretical chances (for example, the possible sums when rolling two number cubes).

Students identify combinations and possible outcomes of multiple-event situations, using tree diagrams and tables. The tree diagram is used as a model to count all possible outcomes. Later the tree diagram is also used to find favorable outcomes in different situations by tracing the paths in the tree diagram.

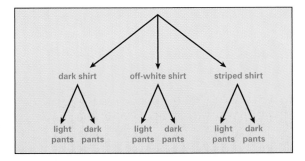

When students have finished this unit, they will:

- understand the meaning of fair and how it relates to chance;
- use tools for making fair decisions;
- understand the meaning of chance or probability;
  - (They understand this at a preformal level. A formal definition of chance is introduced in the unit *Second Chance.*)
- estimate and order chances;
  - (They do this on a preformal level, and on a more formal level in simple situations where they can easily calculate the chances.)
- use repeated trials to estimate chance (experimental chance);
- determine all combinations and possible outcomes using tree diagrams and tables;
- use visual models to estimate and calculate chance;
  - (The models used are chance ladders, chance scales, tree diagrams, and tables. Computing chance is usually done by "counting" in situations with few outcomes.)
- express chance for simple and multiple-event situations using percents, fractions, and ratios; and
- compare theoretical and experimental probability.

Fraction Times

Using survey results for articles in the "Fraction Times" newspaper, students formalize certain operations with fractions and develop their understanding of the relationships between percents, fractions, decimals, and ratios, especially the relationship between part-whole relationships and fractions.

In the context of money, students learn different strategies to multiply whole numbers with decimals, change fractions into decimals and decimals into fractions. Bars and ratio tables are used as tools to compare, add and subtract fractions with different denominators and to simplify fractions.

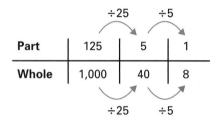

Students use bar models to construct pie charts. The bars and the pie charts also help them to make connections between fractions and percents.

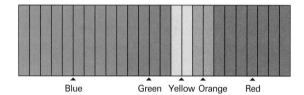

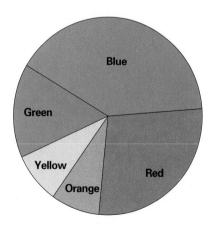

When students have finished this unit, they will have developed:

- number sense and a conceptual understanding of ratios and fractions;
  - Students understand the relationship between part-whole ratios and fractions.
  - They use bars, pie charts, and ratio tables to compare ratios and fractions.
  - They compare, add, subtract, and multiply fractions informally.
  - They find common denominators, using segmented bars and/or ratio tables.
  - They simplify fractions, using a ratio table.
- number sense and a conceptual understanding of decimals; and
  - Students multiply whole numbers with decimals in the context of money.
- number sense and a conceptual understanding of the relationship between ratios, fractions, decimals, and percents.
  - Students choose an appropriate strategy (use benchmark fractions, a ratio table, the context of money, or a calculator) to change a fraction into a decimal or percent.
  - They choose an appropriate strategy (use benchmark fractions, a ratio table, or place value knowledge) to change a decimal into a fraction.
  - They write a ratio as a decimal and a percent using a calculator and estimate a ratio with a fraction, a decimal, or a percent.

Figuring All the Angles

In this unit, students study absolute direction (by using the compass directions north, south, east, and west) and relative direction (for example, South Dakota is south of North Dakota, but it is in the western part of the United States). Students learn how compass directions can be used to find places on a map and in the real world.

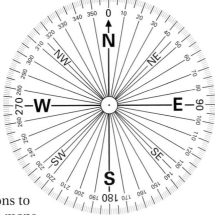

Students locate and give directions to places shown on maps using both compass directions and distances. For that purpose, they are familiarized with the scale line. Also, the difference between distances as the crow flies and taxicab distances becomes clear. Students are familiarized with the compass card and learn how to use headings expressed in degrees for navigation purposes.

Using the polar grid with degrees, students solve problems in which turns are to be made to go from one location to another. The turn is a change of direction. Thus, students are introduced to angles (the turns) in a dynamic way, and the students themselves are the actors (traffic controllers) creating the angles (turns). The context is that of navigation.

When students have finished this unit, they will:

- understand and apply directions;
  - Students use both absolute (compass) and relative directions.
  - They use the concept heading as a direction measured in degrees to the right from the direction north.
  - They informally use a polar grid coordinate system (radar screen) and a rectangular coordinate system (city map) to show directions.
- express distance in different ways;
  - Students express distance as:
    - number of city blocks
    - the crow flies
    - taxicab distance
  - They use a scale line as a representation of distance on a map.
- understand the concept of angles, from informal to formal; and
  - Students look at angles in a dynamic way as turns (changes of direction), as well as in a static way as the result of turns (the track made by a sledge).
  - They estimate angle measurements and measure and draw angles.
  - They discern different types of angles:
    - right angle
    - acute angle
    - obtuse angle
    - straight angle
  - They learn formal notations and terms: vertex, side, ∠A.
  - They explore angles in polygons, interior angles.
  - They are informally introduced to the rules for the sum of angle measurements in a triangle.
- use instruments for angle measurements.
  - Students use a compass card as well as a protractor to measure and draw angles.

Comparing Quantities

This unit introduces students to several informal strategies for solving systems of equations. At the end of the unit, students revisit these problem scenarios more formally as they use variables and formal equations to represent and solve problems.

Variables occur mainly in the role of unknowns. In the beginning of the unit, the variables are presented in pictures. The pictures of the object symbolize a quantity tied to that object. Students operate with pictures in an Algebra sense. At the end of the unit, letters are used to represent the quantities. In between, students can choose their own form of representation: pictures, words, symbols, or letters.

$80.00

$76.00

The principle of fair exchange is visualized in the combination chart. Students identify and use the number patterns in these charts to solve problems.

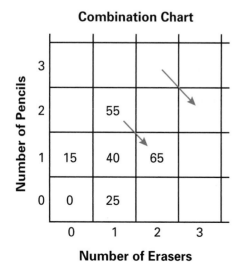

Combination Chart

The notebook notation is based on a matrix with coefficients. This strategy also allows solving sets of equations with more than two variables.

	Apples	Milk	Sandwich	Total	
1	1	0	1	$3.40	
2	0	1	1	$4.20	
3	1	1	0	$2.80	
4	2	2	2	$10.40	row 1 + row 2 + row 3
5	1	1	1	$5.20	row 4 ÷ 2
6	1	0	0	$1.00	row 5 − row 2
7	0	1	0	$1.80	row 3 − row 6
8	0	0	1	$2.40	row 1 − row 6

When students have finished this unit, they will:

- organize information from problem situations;
- have some understanding of the concepts of variable and equation;
- start using symbolic language; and
  - Students use pictures, words, or symbols to describe one's own solution process.
  - They start manipulating with symbols, like A + A + A = 3A.
- informally solve systems of equations.
  - Students use their informal knowledge of bartering and exchanging to solve problems.
  - They produce equivalent equations using pictures, words, symbols, or letters.
  - They follow the solution process of someone else.

Reallotment

In *Reallotment*, students develop an intuitive understanding of area and volume. A process of reallotment (a part that is removed should be made up for elsewhere) becomes a tool students use to find the areas of irregular shapes such as states and irregular polygons. Students develop and use a variety of strategies to find areas and volumes.

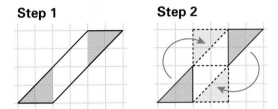

Step 1   **Step 2**

Students develop formal vocabulary related to shapes, area, and volume. They use words such as *length, width, base, height, area, surface area, volume, perimeter, diameter, radius, circumference, square and cubic unit,* and *quadrilateral, parallelogram,* and *prism.*

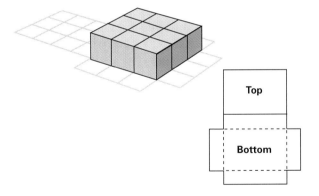

Top

Bottom

When students have finished this unit, they will:

• understand the concepts of area, surface area, and volume;

• use informal and preformal strategies that involve transformations to estimate and compute area of irregular shapes as well as area of rectangles, regular polygons, and other polygons;

  • Students can divide shapes into smaller parts for which area is more easily found.

  • They use "realloting" as a way to compute or estimate area.

• They reshape a figure to compute the area.

• They enclose a shape and subtract the extras to find its area.

• They use relationships between shapes to find area.

• use both non-standard units (like triangles or Escher-like patterns) and standard units (like square centimeters or square inches) to measure and describe area;

  • Students know and use relations between units of measure within the metric system and within the customary system.

  • They use measurement units and tools appropriately for lengths, areas, and volumes.

• use formal vocabulary and methods for calculating area;

  • Students use a formula to find the area of rectangles, parallelograms, and triangles.

  • They can use a formula to estimate and calculate the area of a circle.

• estimate and calculate perimeter of shapes and of enlargements of shapes; and

  • Students understand the relationship between perimeter and area, especially what happens when enlarging or reducing the size of a shape.

  • They use both informal as well as formal ways to find perimeters.

  • They use formulas to compute the perimeter of a circle.

• find the volume of shapes using informal as well as formal strategies.

  • Students find volumes by counting "unit" blocks or by reshaping irregular shapes.

  • They compute volumes of blocks using a formula.

  • They know when the formula *Volume = area of slice × height* can be used and they can use it.

  • They understand the relationship between volume, and surface area.

More or Less

More or Less helps students formalize, connect, and expand their knowledge of fractions, decimals, and percents in number and geometry contexts. Problems involving the multiplication of decimals and percents are introduced.

Students use benchmark fractions to find percents and discounts and use one-step multiplication calculations to compute sale prices and prices that include tax. Arrow strings are used to find the dimensions of enlarged or reduced photocopies and to connect the percent decrease and increase to multiplication.

original length $\xrightarrow{\;\times\cdots\;}$ .... $\xrightarrow{\;\times\cdots\;}$ enlarged length

In this unit, the number models are reviewed. The double number line and the percent bar are especially used to give visual support. In this unit, students use the double number line to calculate the cost of produce. The percent bar helps students connect fractions and percents. To calculate a percent increase or decrease there are many tools students can use: a ratio table, a percent bar, a double number line, or arrow strings.

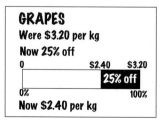

When students have finished this unit, they will have:

- developed number sense and a conceptual understanding of ratios;
  - Students use an estimation strategy to find the cost of produce, for example, by rounding decimals to whole numbers by using benchmark fractions like halves or quarters.
  - They use an exact calculation to find the cost of produce, for example, by changing the decimal numbers into fractions or by using a calculator.
- developed number sense and a conceptual understanding of percents; and
  - Students calculate the sale price of an item with a discount given as a percent or fraction.
  - They start to use multiplication in percent decrease situations, for example, to find the sale price of an item with a discount given as a percent or fraction.
  - They understand that increasing a price by a certain percent is the same as taking 100% plus that percent of the price; for example, increasing a price by 50% is the same as finding 150% of that price.
  - They start to use multiplication in situations of a percent increase, for example, when finding the total price of an item sales tax included or the dimensions of an enlarged picture.
- developed number sense and a conceptual understanding of fractions, decimals, percents, and ratios.
  - Students multiply fractions and decimals.
  - They understand and use benchmark fractions and their relation to ratios, percents, and decimals.
  - They use the relationship of ratios, percents, and decimals to solve problems.
  - They choose an appropriate model or tool to solve problems where fractions, decimals, percents, and ratios are involved (a ratio table, a percent bar, a double number line, arrow strings, a calculator).

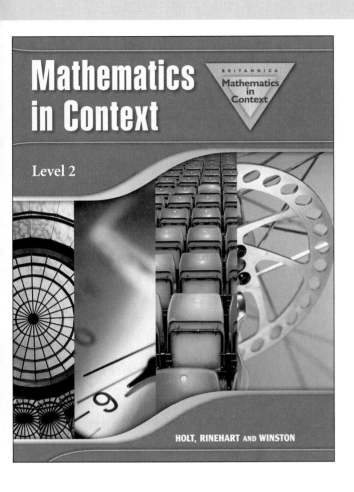

Level 2: Order of Implementation and Pacing Guide

Facts and Factors   **16 days**

Place value, number theory; exponential notation

Dealing with Data   **16 days**

Measures of center; displays of data; sampling techniques

Made to Measure   **14 days**

Estimating and measuring length, area, and volume

Operations   **15 days**

Integers, order of operations; coordinate systems

Packages and Polygons   **19 days**

Two-dimensional representations of three-dimensional prisms; Euler's formula

Ratios and Rates   **18 days**

Ratios, fractions, decimals, and percents as linear functions; scale factors

Building Formulas   **17 days**

Patterns that lead to recursive and direct formulas; equivalent expressions; squares and square roots.

Triangles and Beyond   **18 days**

Transformations, congruence; constructions

Second Chance   **18 days**

Theoretical and experimental probabilities; determining chance

Total days for teaching these units   **151 days**

Facts and Factors

This unit helps students get a better understanding of the base-ten number system and uses the powers of 10 (1, 10, 100, 1,000, and so on) to help students understand and compare the magnitude of very large numbers.

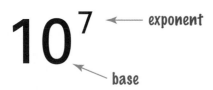

Students investigate divisibility and use different strategies to find the factors of numbers. They are introduced to prime numbers and composite numbers. Students use a factor tree to find the prime factors, and they write numbers as a product of prime factors.

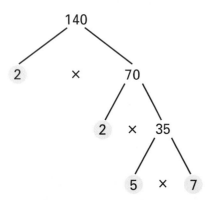

Using the sides and area of a square of graph paper, students explore the relationship between squares and square roots, which leads them to further investigate irrational numbers. Students are formally introduced to square roots and the $\sqrt{}$ symbol.

The area model is developed and used to promote student understanding of how to multiply fractions and mixed numbers.

When students have finished this unit, they will have further developed:

- their number sense and have a conceptual understanding of large numbers, powers, factors, prime numbers;
  - Students understand place value (base ten).
  - They understand exponential notation.
  - They interpret a large number shown on a calculator as a product of a number and a positive power of 10 and write this product as a single number.
  - They explore and understand the binary system.
  - They understand prime and composite numbers.
  - They understand factors and divisors of a number.
- their conceptual understanding of number operations;
  - Students recognize that division and multiplication are related.
  - They apply divisibility rules, for example, divisible by 2, 3, 5, or 9.
  - They use a strategy to completely factor a number into a product of primes.
  - They understand and use informal rules for operations with powers.
  - They square and "unsquare" numbers within the context of area.
  - They use calculators to find square roots.
  - They use the area model to calculate a fraction of a fraction (for example, $\frac{1}{2} \times \frac{1}{2}$, or $\frac{1}{2} \times \frac{1}{4}$).
  - They multiply simple mixed numbers (for example, $3\frac{1}{2} \times 3\frac{1}{2}$, or $(4\frac{1}{2})^2$, or $3\frac{1}{2} \times (6\frac{1}{2})$.

Dealing with Data

In this unit, students are introduced to different ways of organizing and interpreting large sets of data. Using sets of data, including data they collect themselves, students read graphs and interpret scatter plots, stem-and-leaf plots, dot plots on a number line, histograms, and box plots.

Presidents' Ages at Inauguration
4 | 9 8 6 9 7 2
5 | 7 7 7 8 7 4 1 0 2 6 4 1 5 5 4 1 6 5 1 4 1
6 | 1 1 8 4 5
Key: 5 | 7 means 57 years

They study data collection methods and are introduced to the concept of *sample*. Students look for relationships among variables and study patterns in data sets. They calculate the *mean*, *mode*, and *median* and relate these measures of central tendency to graphs representing the same data.

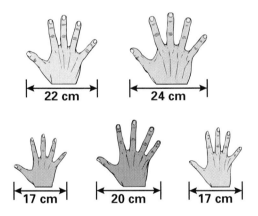

When students have finished this unit, they will:

- create and interpret different kinds of graphs: scatter plots, box plots, stem-and-leaf plots, histograms, and number line plots;
  - Students are introduced to these types of graphs in this unit. These graphs will also be revisited in the unit *Insights into Data*.
- collect data and represent them in tabular and graphic form;
  - Students create their own diagrams as well as make stem-and-leaf plots, scatter plots, histograms, number line plots, and box plots.
  - They identify advantages and disadvantages of different graphical representations.
- describe data numerically using mean, median, mode, quartile, range, maximum, and minimum;
  - Students know different ways to find these descriptive statistics from a given data set.
  - They are able to tell whether mean, mode, or median, together with measures of spread, are useful for describing a given data set.
- understand the concepts of representative sample and population; and
  - These concepts are introduced here and are revisited and formalized in the units *Insights into Data* and *Great Expectations*.
- use data, graphs, and numeric characteristics to build arguments and compare data sets.
  - Students can see patterns and other features of datasets in graphs and other diagrams.

Made to Measure

Students work with metric and customary units to make actual measurements for length, area, and volume. They begin by studying historic units of measure based on body parts, such as *foot*, *pace*, and *fathom* (length of outstretched arms). By comparing historic units of measurement to standardized ones, students understand the importance of the use of standard measurement units.

When solving problems, students need to decide whether an estimated answer, using estimation rules for conversion, is sufficient or if an exact answer is needed. If an exact answer is needed, they must decide how many decimals are appropriate in the realistic situation they are dealing with.

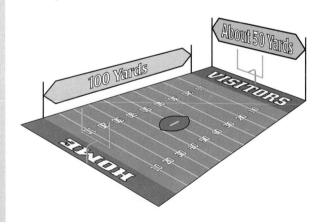

When students have finished this unit, they will:

- measure length, area, and volume, using metric and customary units of measure;
  - Students understand how historic units of measure relate to body measures.
  - They understand the importance of the use of standardized measurement units.
  - They convert units from one measurement system to the other and within systems.
  - They find their own points of reference when using estimation rules to make mental computations easier.
  - They choose appropriate units of measurement in a situation.
  - They decide whether an exact measure or an estimated one is appropriate in a situation.
- use and critique mathematical models to represent an irregular shape;
  - Students use and compare a variety of models to find the body's surface area.
  - They use a cylinder filled with water to find the volume of a hand.
- use the formula *Volume = area of base × height* to find the volume of some objects;
- use tools like centimeter rulers or inch rulers and compass cards and protractors; and
  - Students measure and draw angles using appropriate units.
  - They use a nomogram to relate a body's surface area to a person's height and weight.
- solve problems in a variety of situations involving length, area, and volume.
  - Students investigate the relationship between foot length and shoe size.
  - They investigate the relationship between fathom and height.
  - They use geometric models to solve problems like the angle between back rest and seat of a chair.

Operations

Negative numbers are used by students to model a variety of situations. Starting with the concept of positive and negative numbers in different contexts, like time zones and below and above sea level, informal addition and subtraction of integers is introduced.

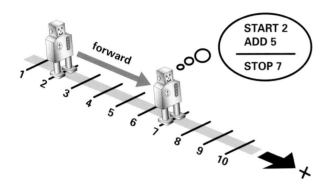

Before starting with multiplication of integers, students have many opportunities to practice adding and subtracting integers in many different ways. Multiplication is introduced using a double number line.

Students plot and interpret points on the coordinate plane. Rules for operations with integers are reinforced by performing transformations of geometric shapes on the coordinate system.

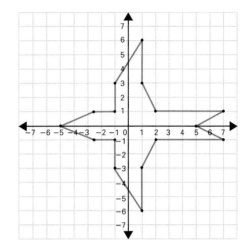

When students have finished this unit, they will:

- understand the concept of integers;
  - Students are able to use integers in many different situations.
- compare and order positive and negative numbers;
  - Students understand and use formal symbols < and >.
  - They order numbers on a number line.
- perform operations with integers;
- understand and use a coordinate system; and
  - Students transform figures in a coordinate system.
- calculate the arithmetic mean of a data set by looking at deviations to introduce formal multiplication using integers.

Packages and Polygons

This unit focuses on developing students' spatial sense. It deepens and formalizes students' knowledge of the structure and characteristics of two- and three-dimensional geometric shapes. Students begin by sorting common objects by shape. They learn the names of solids, including *sphere, cone, truncated cone, prism, right rectangular prism, cube, cylinder,* and *pyramid.* They also identify the attributes of these solids and identify the solids in common objects.

Students build paper models using nets, and they build bar models using toothpicks and gumdrops. Nets are used to explain the concept of a face. Bar models show the concept of edges (the toothpicks) and the concept of vertices (the gumdrops).

Students revisit the formula *Volume = area of slice × height* from the unit *Reallotment* and use it to calculate the volume of a cylinder. Students explore the relationship between the volume of a pyramid and the rectangular prism that has the same base and height.

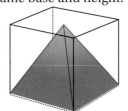

When students have finished this unit, they will have further developed:

- their knowledge and understanding of shapes and construction and developed spatial sense;
  - Students differentiate between two-dimensional shapes and three-dimensional shapes.
  - They identify three dimensional shapes.
  - They identify edges, vertices, and faces.
  - They understand stability of two- and three-dimensional shapes, for example, cylinder, sphere, cone, triangular prism, rectangular solid, and pyramid.
  - They identify polygons as two-dimensional shapes and regular polygons, for example, equilateral triangle, pentagon.
  - They use nets to construct three-dimensional models of geometric shape.
  - They solve three dimensional problems using two-dimensional representations (nets) or reasoning.
  - They identify regular polyhedra.
  - They understand and use Euler's formula.

- their understanding of measurement.
  - Students choose a strategy to find measurements of the angles of a regular polygon.
  - They further develop the concept of volume.
  - They investigate and understand the relationship between liters and cubic centimeters.
  - They use strategies that involve transformations of three-dimensional shapes to estimate and compute volume.
  - They measure the height of a three-dimensional shape.
  - They understand and use the formula *Volume = area of slice × height.*
  - They calculate the volume of cylinders and pyramids.
  - They calculate the volume of a pyramid and a cone.

Ratios and Rates

This unit focuses on the connections between different types of rational numbers and percents. *Ratios and Rates* extends students' understanding of ratio. Ratio tables help students understand that ratios are also averages. When they start to compare ratios, the terms *relative comparison* and *absolute comparison* are introduced, and students discover the value of comparing ratios (for example, number of telephone numbers to number of people) as opposed to looking only at amounts (such as number of telephone numbers).

Students revisit the use of number models from earlier units. They investigate scale lines on a map and find the scale ratio of a map using a double number line. They use arrow strings in situations of enlargements and reductions.

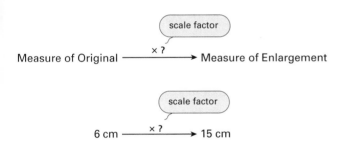

Students use ratio tables to find single number ratios to make relative comparisons and to find a scale factor or to solve problems about enlargements and reductions.

Miles	50	100	20	
Gallons	2.5	5	1	

When students have finished this unit, they will have developed:

- number sense and a conceptual understanding of fractions, decimals, percents, and ratios;
  - Students relate ratios to fractions, decimals, and percents.
  - They divide by decimals.
  - They informally make connections between operations and fractions, for example, a length × 0.25 is the same as a length ÷ 4.
- number sense and a conceptual understanding of ratios;
  - Students start to use ratio tables to compare ratios.
  - They understand problems with part-part ratios versus part-whole ratios.
  - They understand the notion of rate or ratio as an average.
  - They use a scale line on a map.
  - They start to make connections between scale ratios and scale lines on maps.
  - They understand scale factor.
  - They use a scale factor to find actual sizes in situations of reductions and enlargements.
  - They find the scale factor using an actual length and an enlarged (or reduced) size.
- large number sense; and
  - Students compare large numbers.
  - They understand and use million and billion as a kind of measure, for example, when they compare 150 million to 1.2 billion.
- measurement sense.
  - Students use centimeters or millimeters to measure distances.
  - They review relationships between metric units, for example, meters and centimeters, and kilometers and meters.

Building Formulas

Students make and use formulas to further develop the concepts and skills introduced in previous Algebra units. They extend and represent geometric patterns using tables and formulas and graphs. Understanding how formulas are built and how the meaning of the variables relate to the geometric patterns is stressed, more than performing formal operations with expressions and formulas.

Students expand their understanding of the order of operations using parentheses. They also encounter the distributive property informally as they describe repeating brick patterns for a garden border.

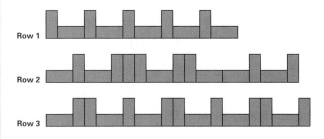

Students square and "unsquare" numbers and express this using arrow strings. They use formulas for surface area and volume introduced in the Geometry unit *Reallotment*.

When students have finished this unit, they will:

- describe patterns in a table, formula, and graph;
  - Students represent a visual pattern with words, symbols, and numbers.
  - They understand and use recursive and direct formulas.
  - They use and generate tables and graphs.
  - They recognize relationships among representations (tables, graphs, and formulas) and discuss advantages and disadvantages of each.

- understand the distributive property and the use of parentheses in general; and
  - Students do this in a preformal way.
  - They understand the concept of equivalent expressions in a preformal way without memorizing a formal definition.

- use formulas to solve a variety of real world problems.
  - Students organize and choose appropriate representations for the information from a problem situation.
  - They know how to criticize and if necessary rewrite a given formula
  - They make a transition from the mathematical model to the realistic problem situation and adjust results accordingly.
  - They round off an answer finding a "reasonable" number of decimals according to the situation.
  - They apply their knowledge of square numbers and roots when using formulas for surface area and volume.

Triangles and Beyond

In this unit, students develop a more formal understanding of the properties of triangles. They also develop a more formal understanding of *parallel* and define *parallelogram, rectangle, rhombus,* and *square* in their own words.

After identifying triangles in their surroundings, students try to make triangles with various sets of three sticks of different lengths. Students learn to construct triangles given the length of the sides using a pair of compasses. Students classify triangles according to their side length and according to their angles.

When students make triangles using squares, they discover that a right triangle is formed only when the sum of the areas of the two smaller squares equals the area of the largest square. In this unit, the Pythagorean theorem is not formally stated as $a^2 + b^2 = c^2$.

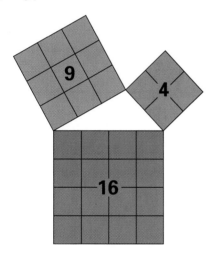

Given definitions for the terms *congruent, translation, rotation,* and *reflection,* students use animal stamps and their own designs to gain informal experience with these concepts. Translations are combined to construct regular polygons, parallelograms, and rectangles.

When students have finished this unit, they will:

- recognize and classify triangles (equilateral, isosceles, and scalene triangles; right, acute, and obtuse triangles) and quadrilaterals (parallelogram, rectangle, rhombus, and square);

- understand the concept of parallel lines, the Pythagorean theorem, congruent figures, line of symmetry, and transformations (translations, rotations, and reflections);

- make constructions of triangles given the side lengths and of parallel lines and families of parallel lines; and

- use the properties of triangles and parallel lines to solve problems with the Pythagorean theorem and the rule that the sum of the angle measurements in a triangle is 180°.

Second Chance

Second Chance builds on the preformal notion of chance that students have developed in the unit *Take a Chance*. Students analyze situations, and they collect information about possible outcomes and how often they occur in experiments and surveys. They use this information to make chance statements and to estimate chances.

In the course of this unit, the tree diagram evolves into a chance tree. In a chance tree, not all events connected to the different branches have the same chance of occurring; this is indicated by writing the chances in the tree.

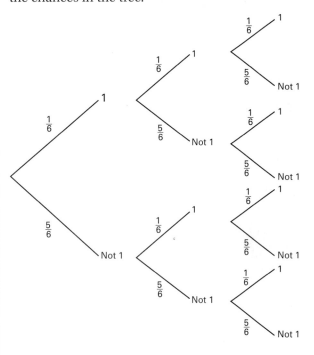

Students use chance trees as well as the area model to compute chances for combined events. The multiplication rule for finding chances of combined events is addressed through the use of these models.

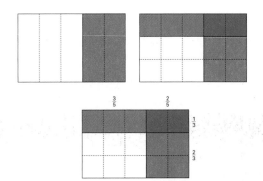

When students have finished this unit, they will:

- understand the meaning of chance or probability;
  - A formal definition of *chance* as the number of favorable outcomes divided by the total number of outcomes is introduced in this unit.

- express chance for combined event situations using ratios, fractions, decimals, or percents;

- determine all possible outcomes and all favorable outcomes (as a subset of these) for situations with combined events, using tree diagrams and tables;

- use visual models to reason about, estimate, and compute chances;
  - The models used are: tree diagram, chart, table, relative frequency graph, histogram, two-way table, chance tree, and area model.

- compute chances;
  - In appropriate situations where all possible outcomes are equally likely, students use the rule: The chance on a certain outcome is the number of favorable outcomes divided by the total number of outcomes.
  - To compute chances for combined (simple compound) events, students use a chance tree or an area model to multiply and add chances.
  - To compute chances from experimental (empirical) data, students use the rule stated above.

- use repeated trials in an experiment or simulation to estimate chance (experimental or empirical chance), based on the recorded results;

- compare theoretical and experimental probability;
  - This is elaborated and formalized in this unit.

- understand that in the long run the chance found in an experimental way will be close to the theoretical chance; and

- use information from two-way tables to decide whether events are related.
  - This is preformal. The terms *dependent* or *independent events* are not yet used; they are introduced in the unit *Great Expectations*.

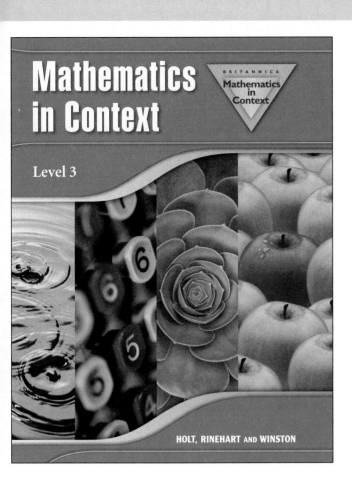

Level 3: Order of Implementation and Pacing Guide

Revisiting Numbers	**15 days**
Scientific notation; unit rates; operations with rational numbers	
Ups and Downs	**18 days**
Exponential functions; tables, graphs, and formulas	
It's All the Same	**17 days**
Congruence and similarity	
Graphing Equations	**18 days**
Slope, tangent, linear equations	
Insights into Data	**18 days**
Statistical measures of data; representations of data; conclusions based on data collection	
Patterns and Figures	**16 days**
Patterns; recursive and direct formulas	
Looking at an Angle	**15 days**
Right triangle relationships; three-dimensional views of two-dimensional drawings	
Great Predictions	**16 days**
Permutations; dependent events; random samples and bias	
Algebra Rules!	**21 days**
Linear functions; factoring; quadratics	
Total days for teaching these units	**154 days**

Unit 19 Overview

Revisiting Numbers

Revisiting Numbers builds on students' previous experience with numbers. Rational number ideas are reviewed, extended, and formalized. Investigations of relationships between operations and their inverses promote understanding of whole numbers, integers, and rational and irrational numbers.

Students review and expand their abilities to operate with fractions and mixed numbers. They use a variety of strategies to solve problems where multiplications and divisions with fractions and mixed numbers are involved, using a double number line, a ratio table, and the area model.

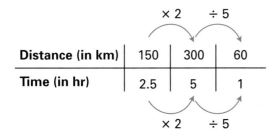

The rules for multiplication with positive and negative numbers are reviewed. Using the between multiplication and division, rules for division with positive and negative numbers are explored and formalized.

Negative exponents are introduced, and two rules for operations with powers of ten are formalized:

If m and n are whole numbers, then $10^m \times 10^n = 10^{m+n}$ and $10^m \div 10^n = 10^{m-m}$. Negative powers of ten are introduced using the patterns in an arrow string that shows the repeated division by ten of the dilution process.

$$10,000 = 10^4$$
$$\downarrow \div 10$$
$$1,000 =$$
$$\downarrow \div 10$$
$$100 =$$
$$\downarrow \div 10$$
$$10 =$$
$$\downarrow \div 10$$
$$1 =$$
$$\downarrow \div 10$$
$$0.1 =$$
$$\downarrow \div 10$$
$$0.01 =$$
$$\downarrow \div 10$$
$$0.001 =$$
$$\downarrow \div 10$$
$$0.0001 =$$

When students have finished the unit, they will have developed:

- number sense and a conceptual understanding of rates and of small and large numbers;
  - Students solve problems about speed rate and change units (for example, from km/h into m/s).
  - They apply their knowledge of place value (base ten).
  - They interpret large and small numbers shown on a calculator as a product of a number and a positive or negative power of 10 and write this product as a single number.
  - They understand and use scientific notation.
- a conceptual understanding of operations; and
  - They recognize relationships among basic operations (for example, division and multiplication, addition and subtraction, square and square roots).
  - They analyze and explain algorithms for multiplication and division.
  - They formalize and use rules for operations with powers, and negative and positive numbers.
  - They understand and use rules for operations (for example, commutative, distributive, and associative, properties).
- a conceptual understanding of different subsets of real numbers.
  - Students understand natural numbers, whole numbers, integers, rational numbers, irrational numbers, and real numbers.
  - They locate real numbers on a number line.

Ups and Downs

In *Ups and Downs*, students graph, describe, and analyze real data about natural phenomena, including data about plant and human growth. More formal mathematical language is used to describe changes in growth. Students are introduced to recursive and direct formulas as tools for investigating linear growth.

Students investigate linear and quadratic growth by looking at the tables, graphs, and formulas that represent different types of growth. The relationship between the different representations is stressed.

Height (in cm)	6	7	8	9	10	11	12
Area (in cm²)	18	24.5	32	...?...	...?...	...?...	...?...

First Difference   6.5   7.5   ..?..   ..?..   ..?..   ..?..

Second Difference   1   1   ..?..   ..?..   ..?..

Students are informally introduced to exponential growth as they examine the growth patterns of bacteria and weeds. Exponential growth can be modeled with repeated multiplication. The *growth factor* is the ratio between the two numbers for adjoining time periods.

Over the course of the unit, students gain an understanding of periodic functions by looking at the rise and fall of tides, changes in blood pressure with heartbeats, and the speed of a car on a racetrack. Exponential decay is addressed within the context of the absorption of medicine in the blood stream.

Minutes after Taking Medicine	0	10	20	30	40	50	60
Medicine in Kendria's Stomach (in mg)	650						

When students have finished this unit, they will:

- understand formal relationships between different representations like description in words, table, equation, and graph;
  - Students use more formal mathematical language to describe patterns, like *constant rate of change, increasing more and more,* and *growth factor.*
  - They understand and use recursive and direct formulas.
- discern different types of graphs; and
  - Line graphs representing information occurring over time, like changes in length of a child, changes in plant growth, and growth of a tree. The graph shows a certain trend but you cannot use one formula or equation to describe it.
  - Straight line, representing a linear function.
  - Periodic graphs.
  - Graphs that show exponential growth or decay.
- discern different types of formulas or equations.
  - Equations describing a linear relationship: rate of change is constant.
  - Equations describing a quadratic relationship: second differences are equal.
  - Informal use of equations for exponential growth or decay. If each value in the table is found by multiplying by a constant growth factor, the growth is exponential.

It's All the Same

In this unit, students investigate the properties of similar triangles at a formal level, and more formal mathematical language is introduced and used throughout this unit. The tessellation, or covering of a surface with congruent figures and cutting the tessellation along parallel lines, is an activity used to introduce the concepts of congruent and similar triangles.

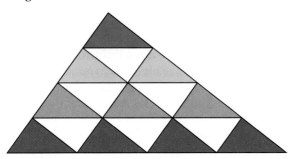

Students apply their knowledge of similar triangles to solve realistic problems, like calculating the height of a bridge above a river, calculating the width of an open stepladder, or building a porch.

In the last section of the unit, students review the concept that parallel lines in a coordinate system have the same slope and that perpendicular lines have slopes that are each other's negative reciprocal. The slopes of lines are, likewise, used to prove whether intersecting lines are perpendicular. Students use the Pythagorean theorem to calculate the lengths of line segments to prove whether or not a quadrilateral is a rhombus and whether the diagonals for a rectangle have the same length. The Pythagorean theorem is also used to calculate the distance between two separate points on a grid.

When students have finished this unit, they will:

- understand and use the concept of congruent and similar figures;
  - Students begin with an informal definition of congruency: congruent figures are exact copies. This is more formalized later as: two figures are congruent if they have the same size and the same shape.
  - They use a multiplication factor to find unknown lengths of similar figures.
  - They develop different strategies to calculate unknown lengths of similar triangles.
  - They express the multiplication factor both as a ratio and a percent.
  - They use formal notations such as ABCD ~ DEFG and learn, for example, that the same angle in triangle DAB can be written as either ∠A or ∠DAB.
  - They know that if triangles are similar, their corresponding sides have the same ratio and their corresponding angles are equal, and vice versa.
- understand the relationship between angles and parallel lines;
  - Students use tessellations to explore intersecting families of parallel lines and find that corresponding and alternate interior angles are equal in size, and vice versa.
- use the properties of similar triangles and parallel lines to solve problems; and
  - Students use these properties to prove, for example, whether a quadrilateral is a rectangle, rhombus, or parallelogram.
- understand and use formal properties of straight lines in a coordinate system.
  - Students use the Pythagorean theorem to calculate the length of line segments and the distance between two separate points in a coordinate system.
  - They use the rule that the sum of the angle measurements in a triangle is 180°.

Graphing Equations

In *Graphing Equations*, students move from locating points using compass directions and bearings to locating points on a coordinate system in the context of a forest fire. They continuously formalize their knowledge, building on the introduction from the unit *Operations* and adopt conventional formal vocabulary and notation, such as *origin, quadrant,* and *x-axis*, as well as the *ordered pairs notation (x, y)*.

The use of the *y*-intercept as a reference point for graphing linear functions is formally introduced in this unit. Students draw lines for given equations and write equations for drawn lines.

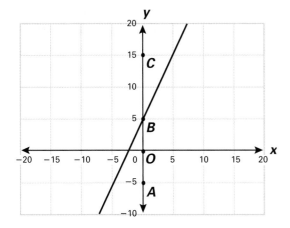

Students study the concept of slope and *y*-intercept and write equations for straight lines. Visualizing frogs jumping toward or away from a path helps students develop formal algebraic methods for solving linear equations. By simultaneously changing the diagrams and the equations the diagram visualizes to solve a problem, students learn to understand and use a formal way of solving equations.

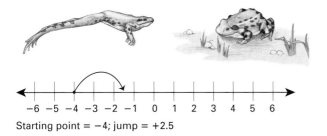

Starting point = −4; jump = +2.5

Students combine the graphic method to find a point of intersection with the use of equations. By linking the lines in the graph to their equations using arrows, the method for solving frog problems is related to finding the point of intersection of two lines. They connect the graphic and algebraic method explicitly for a deeper understanding of the two.

When students have finished this unit, they will:

- understand the use of compass directions and angle measurements;
  - Students revisit the navigation and angle measurement concepts introduced in previous geometry units.
  - They describe directions using ordered number pairs.

- understand the relationship between equation and graph of a linear function; and
  - Students study and use the concept of slope at a more formal level.
  - They understand the relationship between slope and tangent ratio of a line.
  - They graph points and lines in a coordinate system.
  - They find the *y*-intercept using the equation of a line or the graph and understanding its meaning.
  - They find and use equations of a straight line.
  - They use inequalities to describe a region.
  - They find the intersection point of two straight lines by reading from the graph and checking as well as by solving a linear equation.
  - They understand similarities between graphic and algebraic strategies.

- solve single variable linear equations.
  - Students write and solve linear equations.

Insights into Data

Insights into Data encourages students to think critically about representing and analyzing data. It builds on graphical representations of data and numerical measures of data introduced and used in the units *Picturing Numbers* and *Dealing with Data.*

Students conduct their own experiment in which they measure and record the growth of mung beans watered with tap water and three other solutions. Later in the unit, they present their own bean sprout data. They organize, depict, and describe these data and present the findings on plant growth in a report. They use stem-and-leaf plots, box plots, coordinate systems, or histograms in their report.

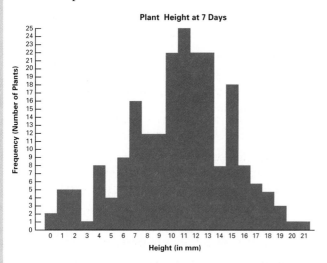

Students study patterns in data. They do so, for example, in a scatter plot in the context of per capita income data connected to data on percent of population living in urban areas per state. Students are preformally introduced to terms like *cluster* and *outliers.*

By studying a variety of graphs, students discover ways in which graphic displays can give different impressions or even be misleading.

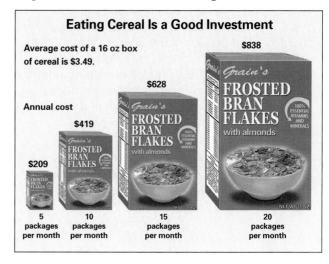

When students have finished this unit, they will:

• understand graphical representations of data such as: scatter plots, box plots, number line plots, stem-and-leaf plots, and histograms.;

• identify the misrepresentation of data and correct it (if possible);

• reason about (random) sampling and describe possible causes for bias in the process of sampling and survey results;

• describe how to choose a fair or good sample of a population;

• collect data through survey, experiment, and simulation;

• represent data graphically and describe data with statistical measures (mean, median, and mode);

• describe a correlation in a scatter plot in preformal terms like: *weak, moderate, strong, positive, negative, linear, non-linear*;

• draw straight lines that summarize data and use the equations of these lines to predict outcomes;

• describe the meaning of the slope and the *y*-intercept of the line in terms of the context; and

• draw conclusions based on data and representations of data.

Patterns and Figures

In *Patterns and Figures*, students study sequences and the recursive and direct formulas that describe them. Students investigate the use of number strips and dot patterns to represent number sequences. Students write the recursive and direct formulas that describe them. Students use number strips to combine sequences by addition and subtraction and find resulting expressions.

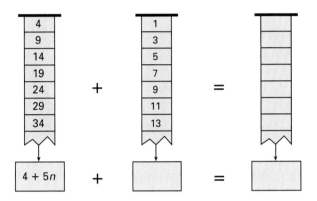

The area model and number strips are used to introduce square numbers and quadratic expressions.

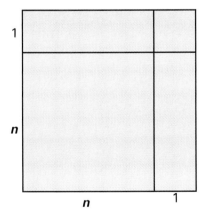

Students also encounter or revisit other important mathematical topics such as rectangular and triangular numbers. Tessellations, stacks of cans or pipes, and a ping-pong competition are used for these number patterns. This unit makes connections between algebra and geometry.

When students have finished this unit, they will:

- describe patterns in a sequence of numbers and shapes using words, number strips, and formulas to describe them;

  - Students create and use NEXT-CURRENT and direct formulas (formal).

  - They use an expression to find the connecting sequence.

  - They more formally understand the concept of equivalent formulas and expressions.

  - They know that an arithmetic sequence shows constant increase or decrease.

  - They use odd and even numbers.

  - They use dot patterns and expressions to describe a sequence of square numbers

- make connections between algebra and geometry, using "geometric algebra."

  - Students use dot patterns to describe increase in the sequence of square numbers. They informally explore 1st and 2nd differences.

  - They use area diagrams and number strips to find equivalent expressions for expressions such as $(2\frac{1}{2})^2$; $(n + 1)^2$; $(2n + 1)^2$.

  - They explore the properties of triangular and rectangular numbers.

  - They use geometric representations to show that the nth rectangular number can be described by $n(n + 1)$, n starts at 1; and the nth triangular number can be described by $n(n + 1)$, n starts at 1.

Looking at an Angle

In *Looking at an Angle,* the last unit of the Geometry strand, different concepts are formalized. Investigating a model of the Grand Canyon, students identify lines of sight, or vision lines. They figure out, for example, from which places on the rim of the Grand Canyon the river can be seen and why it cannot be seen from other vantage points. Then they use vision lines to determine the blind spot of the captain of different ships from which a swimmer or small boat will not be seen

Captain

The path of a hang glider is used to introduce the tangent ratio and to formalize students' understanding of it. Students compare the performance of different hang gliders by considering their glide ratio. They learn how glide ratios can also be expressed as fractions or decimals. Students' understanding of the glide ratio is formalized as the tangent ratio, which they use to solve problems.

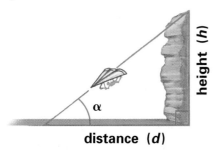

height (*h*)

α

distance (*d*)

The steepness of a vision line, of the sun's rays, of a ladder, and of the flight path of a hang glider can all be modeled by a right triangle. This leads to formalization of the use of the Pythagorean theorem and its reverse. Students also learn about two other ratios between the sides of a right triangle, the sine and the cosine, which are then used in solving problems.

When students have finished this unit, they will:

- understand and use the concept of vision lines;
  - Students model situations and solve problems involving vision lines, blind spots, and blind areas.
  - They understand the relationship between vision lines and blind spots, and the sun's rays and shadows.
  - They understand the difference between shadows caused by the sun and shadows caused by a nearby light source.

- understand and use the concept of tangent, sine and cosine; and
  - Students use previous knowledge of ratio, proportion, angle, and angle measure.
  - They develop informal understanding of tangent ratio by studying blind spots, shadows, steepness, and glide ratios.
  - They develop formal notation and solve problems involving tangent, sine and cosine.
  - They use a calculator to find the tangent of an angle and the reverse operation.
  - They explore the relationship between slope and glide ratio (tan α).

- know and use the Pythagorean theorem and its inverse.

Great Predictions

The unit *Great Predictions* is the last unit in the Data Analysis and Probability strand. It combines concepts from data analysis and from probability. The unit explores representative and biased samples, dependent and independent events, expected values, and joint probability.

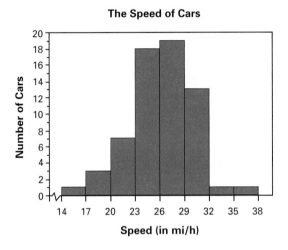

The Speed of Cars

Students learn that drawing conclusions from samples always involves uncertainty. They experience that small samples can have variability. Combining results of samples taken by a whole class helps students realize that variability can get smaller if samples get bigger and that a larger sample is more likely to be representative of the population.

An opinion poll about building a bridge across a river formally introduces the concepts of dependent and independent events. Students use tree diagrams, chance trees, and tables to organize information and make inferences about whether events seem to be dependent or not.

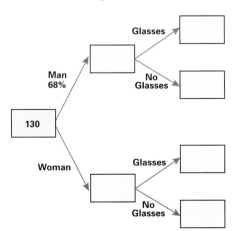

When students have finished this unit, they will:

- understand the relationship between a sample and a population;

  - Students draw conclusions from samples, and they know that uncertainty or chance is involved when doing this.

  - They know that samples must be large enough and randomly chosen to give a good image of the population.

  - They understand the concepts of randomness and bias.

- understand the difference between independent and dependent events;

  - Students use information from two-way tables or tree diagrams to decide whether events are dependent or independent.

  - They understand that if events are dependent, this does not tell why a connection exists. This may be due to chance.

- calculate and use expected value to make decisions;

  - Expected value is introduced in this unit.

  - Students calculate expected value from a chance tree or a table.

- understand the meaning of chance or probability, and they estimate and compute chances; and

  - Students find chances as relative frequencies from tables and graphs.

  - They calculate chances in multi- event situations using chance trees or an area model.

    Note: These models were introduced and used in the units *Take a Chance* and *Second Chance*.

  - The multiplication rule for chances (for independent events) is formalized in this unit.

- make connections between statistics and probability.

  - Students use data to compute chances.

Algebra Rules!

This capstone algebra unit brings together and formalizes the substrands Processes, Restrictions, and Patterns that were introduced and developed in previous units. More formal mathematical language is used. The associative, commutative properties of addition and multiplication and the distributive property are used implicitly.

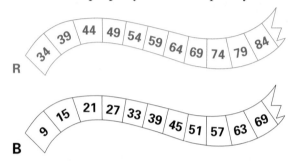

An important goal for this unit is for students to become flexible in working with expressions and be aware of the relationships between different representations. Students perform operations with linear expressions at the level of mastery. They are introduced to performing operations with quadratic expressions.

Linear functions are considered in a geometric as well as an algebraic way. The relationship between slope, y-intercept, and x-intercept is addressed.

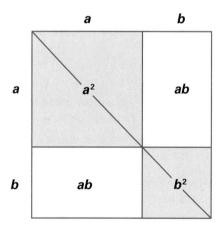

When students have finished this unit, they will:

- connect operations with linear expressions to "Number Strips," arithmetic sequences in mathematical language;

- use the linear function, which is the continuous counterpart of arithmetic sequences;
  - Students recognize how different (word) formulas they have seen before are all part of the same "family" of linear relationships.
  - They recognize linearity from a graph, a table, and a formula and can graph linear functions.
  - The concept of x-intercept is added to the concepts of slope and y-intercept.

- use a graphing calculator when appropriate (optional);

- solve linear equations and operate with expressions;
  - The "difference is zero" method is introduced: A = B if and only if A − B = 0.
  - Relate linear graphs to the solution of a linear equation.

- perform operations with graphs: adding, subtracting, and multiplying with a constant; these operations are also turned into operations with expressions;

- use the rectangle model to explain and use the distributive property; and

- begin to use informal operations with quadratic forms.

Additional Materials

Number Tools

Number Tools is a multi-grade supplement that can be used to provide additional experiences during or after a unit and to develop prerequisite skills for other units.

The activities can be used for intervention sheets or practice pages to support the development of basic skills and number sense in the areas of ratio, fractions, decimals, and percents, and the connections between these representations. *Number Tools* is available as a set of blackline masters with solutions or as a consumable Student Workbook without solutions.

Algebra Tools

The *Algebra Tools* workbook provides materials for additional practice and further exploration of algebraic concepts and skills that can be used in conjunction with units of the Algebra strand or independently from individual units. *Algebra Tools* is available as a set of blackline masters with solutions or as a consumable Student Workbook without solutions.

Manipulatives Kit

The Manipulatives Kit provides adequate materials for a class of 32 students. One kit is designed for use at all grade levels; this is especially convenient for teachers who teach multiple grade levels or who have small classes and want to share with a colleague. Included in the kit are compass cards, rulers, protractors, compasses, measurement instruments for liquid measure, geometric solids, meter sticks, number cubes, and other miscellaneous items. These items are conveniently packaged in a plastic storage container.

Teaching Transparencies

All **Student Activity Sheets** are included as transparencies. In addition, selected charts, graphs, tables, maps, and other teaching tools are included as full-color transparencies. A binder is provided for storage and ease of use.

Mathematics in Context Online

MiC Online is a set of rich, balanced resources for teachers, students, and families. For home use, it includes additional information, activities, tools, skills practice, review, and support to further students' mathematical understanding and achievements. For teachers, it includes lesson plans, unit descriptions, links to state assessment practice, and helpful hints. MiC events and workshops announcements will also be included on the site.

Test and Practice Generator

As a convenience to teachers, this product allows teachers to produce their own tests, quizzes, and practice worksheets from a comprehensive bank of questions aligned with MiC. Since all grade levels will be included on one CD, it also allows teachers to review and enrich through assessment items.

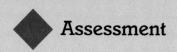

This is a sample (first page) of the Assessment Overview found in the Teacher's Guide for each MiC Unit.

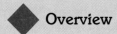

Overview

Student Assessment in Mathematics in Context

As recommended by the NCTM *Principles and Standards for School Mathematics* and research on student learning, classroom assessment should be based on evidence drawn from several sources. An assessment plan for a *Mathematics in Context* unit may draw from the following overlapping sources:

- **observation—As students work individually or in groups, watch for evidence of their understanding of the mathematics.**
- **interactive responses—Listen closely to how students respond to your questions and to the responses of other students.**
- **products—Look for clarity and quality of thought in students' solutions to problems completed in class, homework, extensions, projects, quizzes, and tests.**

Assessment Pyramid

When designing a comprehensive assessment program, the assessment tasks used should be distributed across the following three dimensions: mathematics content, levels of reasoning, and difficulty level. The Assessment Pyramid, based on Jan de Lange's theory of assessment, is a model used to suggest how items should be distributed across these three dimensions. Over time, assessment questions should "fill" the pyramid.

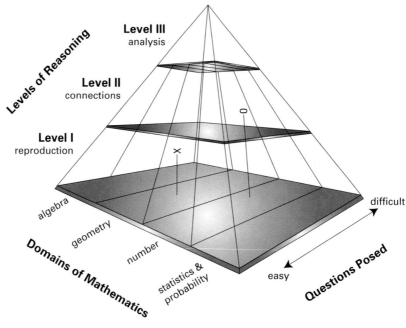

This is a sample (second page) of the Assessment Overview found in the Teacher's Guide for each MiC Unit.

Overview

Levels of Reasoning

Level I questions typically address:

- recall of facts and definitions and
- use of technical skills, tools, and standard algorithms.

As shown in the pyramid, Level I questions are not necessarily easy. For example, Level I questions may involve complicated computation problems. In general, Level I questions assess basic knowledge and procedures that may have been emphasized during instruction. The format for this type of question is usually short answer, fill-in, or multiple choice. On a quiz or test, Level I questions closely resemble questions that are regularly found in a given unit substituted with different numbers and/or contexts.

Level II questions require students to:

- integrate information;
- decide which mathematical models or tools to use for a given situation; and
- solve unfamiliar problems in a context, based on the mathematical content of the unit.

Level II questions are typically written to elicit short or extended responses. Students choose their own strategies, use a variety of mathematical models, and explain how they solved a problem.

Level III questions require students to:

- make their own assumptions to solve open-ended problems;
- analyze, interpret, synthesize, reflect; and
- develop one's own strategies or mathematical models.

Level III questions are always open-ended problems. Often, more than one answer is possible and there is a wide variation in reasoning and explanations. There are limitations to the type of Level III problems that students can be reasonably expected to respond to on time-restricted tests.

The instructional decisions a teacher makes as he or she progresses through a unit may influence the level of reasoning required to solve problems. If a method of problem solving required to solve a Level III problem is repeatedly emphasized during instruction, the level of reasoning required to solve a Level II or III problem may be reduced to recall knowledge, or Level I reasoning. A student who does not master a specific algorithm during a unit but solves a problem correctly using his or her own invented strategy may demonstrate higher-level reasoning than a student who memorizes and applies an algorithm.

The "volume" represented by each level of the Assessment Pyramid serves as a guideline for the distribution of problems and use of score points over the three reasoning levels.

These assessment design principles are used throughout *Mathematics in Context*. The Goals and Assessment charts that highlight ongoing assessment opportunities—on pages xvi and xvii of each Teacher's Guide—are organized according to levels of reasoning.

In the Lesson Notes section of the Teacher's Guide, ongoing assessment opportunities are also shown in the Assessment Pyramid icon located at the bottom of the Notes column.

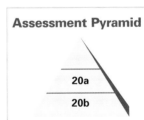

Assessment Pyramid

20a

20b

Interpret the work of other students.

Find all factors for a number from 1 to 100.

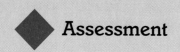

Assessment

Notice the sample of the first page of the Unit Test from the unit *Expressions and Formulas* as well as the Solution and Scoring Guide provided for that page.

◆ Name _____ Date _____

Expressions and Formulas Unit Test

Use additional paper as needed.

1. a. Compute 28 − (2 + 9) and 28 − 2 + 9.

b. Explain why the two answers are different.

c. Rewrite the calculation 15 × 6 + 20 × 5 using parentheses, so that the answer is 550.

2. Design an arithmetic tree that makes these problems easier to solve. Show your work for each problem.

a. 37 + 19 + 12 + 3 + 21 + 8

b. $\frac{1}{8} + \frac{3}{10} + \frac{1}{10} + \frac{7}{8} + \frac{3}{5}$

c. 3.7 + 4.5 − 2.5 + 2.3 + 10

Fast Cab

The meters in the cars of Fast Cab Company calculate the cost of a ride using the following formula.

total price (in dollars) = 3.50 + 1.50 × number of miles

3. a. Explain what the numbers used in the formula mean.

b. Write the formula as an arrow string.

© Encyclopædia Britannica, Inc. This page may be reproduced for classroom use.

This is a sample of the Solution and Scoring Guide provided for the first page of the Unit Test from the unit *Expressions and Formulas.*

◆ **Expressions and Formulas Unit Test**
Solution and Scoring Guide

Possible student answer	Suggested number of score points	Problem level
1. a. $28 - (2 + 9) = 28 - 11 = 17$ $28 - 2 + 9 = 26 + 9 = 35$	2	I
b. Sample student answers: • The order of the operations is different for both computations, because of the parentheses. • In the first computation, you have to calculate $2 + 9$ first, because of the parentheses, and subtract the result from 28. In the second computation, you subtract 2 and add 9.	1	I
c. $(15 \times 6 + 20) \times 5$ or $((15 \times 6) + 20) \times 5$	1	I
2. Different solutions are possible. Only one example of each is shown. Check the results of the computations. **a.** **b.**	3 (Give a half point for each arithmetic tree that shows matching of "easy pairs" to compute.) (Give a half point for a correct answer.)	I / II I / II

The Philosophy of
Mathematics in Context

The design principles for *Mathematics in Context* are derived from Realistic Mathematics Education (RME). Since 1971, researchers at the Freudenthal Institute have developed this theoretical approach towards the learning and teaching of mathematics. RME incorporates views on what mathematics is, how students learn mathematics, and how mathematics should be taught. The principles that underlie this approach are strongly influenced by Hans Freudenthal's concept of "mathematics as a human activity." From the RME perspective, students are seen as reinventors, with teachers guiding and making conscious to students the mathematization of reality. The process of guided reinvention is supported by student engagement in problem solving, a collective as well as an individual activity, in which whole-class discussions centering on conjecture, explanation, and justification play a crucial role. The instructional guidance of teachers in this process is critical, as teachers gradually introduce and negotiate with the students the meanings and use of conventional mathematical terms, signs, and symbols.

The Realistic Mathematics Education philosophy transfers into a design approach for MiC with the following components:

Developing instruction based in experientially real contexts

The starting point of any instructional sequence should involve situations that are experientially real to students so that they can immediately engage in personally meaningful mathematical activity. Such problems often involve everyday life settings or fictitious scenarios, although mathematics itself can also serve as a context of interest. With experience, parts of mathematics become experientially real to students. Such activities should reflect either real phenomena from which mathematics has developed historically or actual situations and phenomena where further interpretation, study, and analysis require the use of mathematics.

Designing structured sets of instructional activities that reflect and work toward important mathematical goals

A second tenet of RME is that the starting point should also be justifiable in terms of the potential end point of a learning sequence. To accomplish this, the domain needs to be well mapped. This involves identifying the key features and resources of the domain that are important for students to find, discover, use, or even invent for themselves, and then relating them via long learning lines. The situations that serve as starting points for a domain are critical and should continue to function as paradigm cases that involve rich imagery and, thus, anchor students' increasingly abstract activity. The students' initially informal mathematical activity should constitute a basis from which they can abstract and construct increasingly sophisticated mathematical conceptions.

Designing opportunities to build connections between content strands through solving problems that reflect these interconnections

The third tenet of RME is based on the observation that real phenomena, in which mathematical structures and concepts manifest themselves, lead to interconnections within and between content strands as well as connections to other disciplines (for example, biological sciences, physics, sociology, and so on). Although the maps developed for each of the four MiC content strands contain unique terms, signs, and symbols as well as an extended learning line for the strand, instruction in actual classrooms inevitably involves the intertwining of these strands. Problems can often be viewed from multiple viewpoints. For example, a geometric pattern can be expressed using numbers relationships or algebraically.

Recognizing and making use of students' prior conceptions and representations (models) to support the development of more formal mathematics (i.e., progressive formalization), RME's fourth tenet is that instructional sequences should involve activities in which students reveal and create models of their informal mathematical activity.

RME's heuristic for laying out long learning lines for students involves a conjecture about the role that emergent models play in the students' learning, namely that students' models of their informal mathematical activity can evolve into models for increasingly abstract mathematical reasoning. Gravemeijer explained this bottom-up progression in terms of four levels of progressive mathematization (see Figure 1).

At the initial "situational level," the expectation is that students develop interpretations, representations, and strategies appropriate for engaging with a particular problem context. At this level, students create and elaborate symbolic models of their informal mathematical activity, such as drawings, diagrams, tables, and informal notations.

At the "referential level," students create informal *models of* the problem situation. Such *models-of* contain the collective descriptions, concepts, procedures, and strategies that refer to concrete or paradigmatic situations. At the "general level," as a result of generalization, exploration, and reflection, students are expected to mathematize their informal modeling activity and begin to focus on interpretations and solutions independent of situation-specific imagery. Models at this level are considered *models-for* and are used as a basis for reasoning and reflection. The "formal level" involves reasoning with conventional symbols and is no longer dependent on *models-for*.

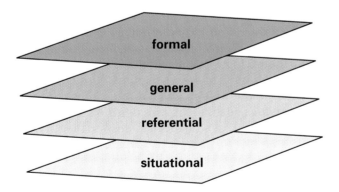

Figure 1.

Thus, for students, a model is first constituted, for example, as a context-specific model of a situation, then generalized across situations. In this process, the model changes in character and becomes an entity in itself, functioning eventually as a basis for mathematical reasoning on a formal level. The development of ways of symbolizing problem situations and the transition from informal to formal notations are important aspects of the selection of problem contexts, the relationships between contexts, and instructional assumptions.

The consequences are that the introduction of numbers, number sentences, standard algorithms, terms, signs and symbols, and the rules of use in formal mathematics should involve a process of *social negotiation* in a manner similar to those from which the notations and rules were derived. In the process of reinventing formal semiotics, students are participating in the human mathematics process of progressive formalization.

The design of activities to promote pedagogical strategies that support students' collective investigation of reality

RME's fifth tenet is that in classrooms the learning process can be effective only when it occurs within the context of interactive instruction. Students are expected to explain and justify their solutions, to work to understand other students' solutions, to agree and disagree openly, to question alternatives, to reflect on what they have discussed and learned, and so on. Creating a classroom that fosters such interaction involves a shift in the teacher's role from dictating the prescribed knowledge via a routine instructional sequence, to orchestrating activities situated in learning trajectories wherein ideas emerge and develop in the social setting of the classroom. To promote the interaction of student representations and strategies, teachers must also create discourse communities that support and encourage student conjectures, modeling, re-modeling, and argumentation.

The development of an assessment system that monitors both group and individual student progress

The teacher's role in the RME instructional process involves capitalizing on students' reasoning and continually introducing and negotiating with students the emergence of shared terms, symbols, rules, and strategies, with an eye to encouraging students to reflect on what they learn. Students are seen as reinventors, with the teacher guiding and making conscious to students the mathematization of reality, with symbolizations emerging and developing meaning in the social situation of the classroom. Students are encouraged to communicate their knowledge, either verbally, in writing, or through some other means like pictures, diagrams, or models to other students and the teacher. Central to this interactive classroom is the development of students' abilities to use mathematical argumentation to support their own conjectures.

A Summary of Implications of Realistic Mathematics Education for MiC

The real-world contexts support and motivate learning.
Mathematics is a tool to help students make sense of their world. *Mathematics in Context* uses real-life situations as a starting point for learning; these situations illustrate the variety of ways in which students can use mathematics. Models help students learn mathematics at different levels of abstraction. The ratio tables, double number lines, chance ladders, percent bars, and other models in *Mathematics in Context* allow students to solve problems at different levels of abstraction. The models also serve as mediating tools between the concrete world of real-life problems and the abstract world of mathematical knowledge.

Students reinvent significant mathematics.
Instruction builds on students' own knowledge of and experiences with mathematics. They serve as a foundation for developing deeper understanding through interaction with other students and the teacher. The teacher's role is to help students make connections and synthesize what they have learned.

Interaction is essential for learning mathematics.
Interaction between teacher and student, student and student, and teacher and teacher is an integral part of creating mathematical knowledge. The problems posed in *Mathematics in Context* provide a natural way for students to interact before, during, and after finding a solution.

Multiple strategies are important.
Most problems can be solved with more than one strategy. *Mathematics in Context* recognizes that students come to each unit with prior knowledge and encourages students to solve problems in their own way—by using their own strategies at their own level of sophistication. It is the teacher's responsibility to orchestrate class discussions to reveal the variety of strategies students are using. Students enrich their understanding of mathematics and increase their ability to select appropriate problem-solving strategies by comparing and analyzing their own and other students' strategies.

Students should not move quickly to the abstract.
In *Mathematics in Context*, it is preferable that students use informal strategies that they understand rather than formal procedures that they do not understand. It is important to allow students to experience and explore concrete mathematics for as long as they need to. Level 1 units offer students an assortment of informal methods for solving problems. Students are given the opportunity to move to more formal strategies in Levels 2 and 3.

Mastery develops over the course of the curriculum.
Because mastery develops over time, teachers should not expect students to master mathematical concepts after a single section or even after a single unit. Each unit is connected to the other units in the curriculum. Through a spiraling of the content and contexts, important mathematical ideas are revisited throughout the curriculum so that students can deepen their understanding and master the ideas over time.

Source: © Rand McNally.

Goals of MiC

The Vision for *Mathematics in Context*

Pedagogically, *Mathematics in Context* is designed to support the National Council of Teachers of Mathematics (NCTM) vision of mathematics education as expressed in the *Principles and Standards for School Mathematics* (NCTM, 2000). It consists of mathematical tasks and questions designed to stimulate mathematical thinking and to promote discussion among students. Students are expected to:

- explore mathematical relationships;
- develop and explain their own reasoning and strategies for solving problems;
- use problem-solving tools appropriately; and
- listen to, understand, and value each other's strategies.

The NCTM *Principles and Standards* state that because mathematical understanding is related to personal experiences in solving problems in the real world, school mathematics is enhanced when it is embedded in realistic contexts that are meaningful to students. *Mathematics in Context* provides these contexts as well as problems that actively engage students in mathematics.

NCTM also suggests that students need ample opportunities to solve realistic problems using strategies that make sense to them. Students must recognize, understand, and extract the mathematical relationships embedded in a broad range of situations. They need to know how to represent quantitative and spatial relationships and how to use the language of mathematics to express these relationships. They must know how and when to use technology. Effective problem-solving also requires the ability to predict and interpret results. *Mathematics in Context* is a connected curriculum that requires students to deepen their understanding of significant mathematics through integrated activities across units and grades.

The History of *Mathematics in Context*

The *Mathematics in Context* curriculum project was initially funded in 1991 by the National Science Foundation to develop a comprehensive mathematics curriculum for the middle grades.

Collaborating on this project were the research and development teams from the National Center for Research in Mathematical Sciences Education (NCRSME) at the University of Wisconsin, Madison, and the Freudenthal Institute (FI) at the University of Utrecht in the Netherlands. Thomas A. Romberg, Project Director, had become familiar with the work of the Freudenthal Institute while chairing the writing team of the NCTM's *Curriculum and Evaluation Standards* (1989). He recognized that the mathematics curriculum used in the Netherlands was consistent with the vision of the Standards and that it could serve as a model for a middle grades curriculum for the United States.

The development of the curriculum units, teacher's guides, and supporting materials took six years (1991–1997). An international advisory committee prepared a blueprint document to guide the development of the curricular materials. Then the Freudenthal Institute staff under the direction of Jan de Lange prepared initial drafts of individual units based upon the blueprint. Researchers at the University of Wisconsin–Madison modified the language and problem contexts in these units to make them appropriate for students and teachers in the United States. Pilot versions of the individual units were tested in middle schools in Wisconsin. Revised field-test versions of the units were created from feedback received during the initial pilot. The revised versions were then used in several states and Puerto Rico. Data from the field-test sites were used to inform revisions to student books and teacher's guides before commercial publication.

The current revision of *Mathematics in Context* (2003–2005) was partially funded by the National Science Foundation. The revision team solicited feedback from experienced MiC teachers. This information was used in conjunction with the NCTM 2000 *Principles and Standards* to shape the changes reflected in the 2006 edition. The staff of the Freudenthal Institute prepared drafts of each revised unit similar to the first edition. The revision team at the University of Wisconsin–Madison then prepared the drafts for field-test, if necessary, and for submission to the publisher. Extensive teacher's guide notes were contributed by experienced MiC teachers.

Student Books

Student Books are available as either individual soft cover non-consumable books or hard-bound by grade level. The soft cover Student Books are three-hole punched for convenient storage in binders.

Letter to the Student introduces the contexts and mathematical concepts for each unit.

Dear Student,

Welcome to *Expressions and Formulas*.

Imagine you are shopping for a new bike. How do you determine the size frame that fits your body best? Bicycle manufacturers have a formula that uses leg length to find the right size bike for each rider. In this unit, you will use this formula as well as many others. You will devise your own formulas by studying the data and processes in the story. Then you will apply your own formula to solve new problems.

In this unit, you will also learn new forms of mathematical writing. You will use arrow strings, arithmetic trees, and parentheses. These new tools will help you interpret problems as well as apply formulas to find problem solutions.

As you study this unit, look for additional formulas in your daily life outside the mathematics classroom, such as the formula for sales tax or cab rates. Formulas are all around us!

Sincerely,

The Mathematics in Context Development Team

Sections Units contain four to eight sections. Each section takes between two and five days to complete. Sections include short descriptions of problem scenarios and related problems for students to solve. Within a section, mathematical concepts are developed but may not be stated explicitly.

Reflect questions ask students to apply higher-order thinking to concepts in the lesson. **Summary** and **Check Your Work** problems allow students to assess their own understanding of the material in the section and to integrate and consolidate what they have learned. Answers to the **Check Your Work** problems are found in the back of the Student Book. This section is also a valuable way to involve families in that the answers allow parents to discuss with their child progress through the unit.

Structure of a Student Book

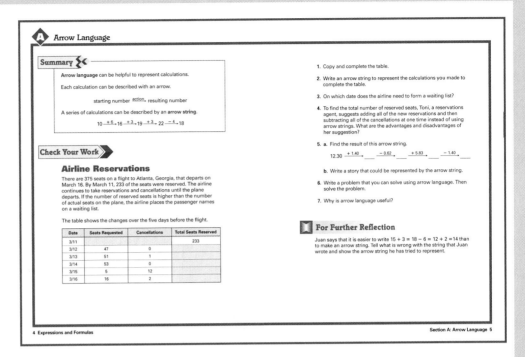

For Further Reflection is the last problem in each section. These problems summarize and discuss important concepts from the section. They ask students to reflect on what they have learned and apply that knowledge to a new situation.

Additional Practice The main concepts of the unit are reinforced by the Additional Practice activities, provided for each section of the unit. They may be used as in-class activities, homework assignments, informal assessment tools, or extra credit.

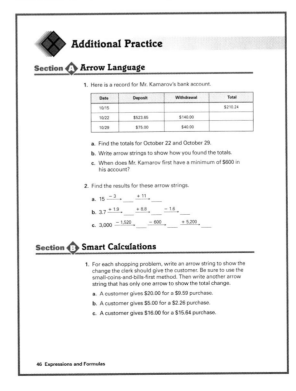

Teacher's Guide

These soft cover books are spiral-bound so that they lay flat when open. Teaching ideas and solutions are conveniently provided adjacent to reduced-sized reproductions of corresponding Student Book pages.

In the Front of the Teacher's Guide

Overview General information about the curriculum as well as unit-specific planning information introduces each unit.

- **Correlation** of the content of the unit with the content standards and expectations of the NCTM Principles and Standards for School Mathematics.

- **Math in the Unit** describes the mathematical content of the unit as well as prior knowledge required of students and student learning expectations.

- **Strand Overview** offers teachers a guide to the development of concepts throughout the strand across all levels.

- **Student Assessment in *Mathematics in Context*** describes the design of the assessment program for MiC. It also explains the important levels of assessment items based on the Assessment Pyramid.

- **Goals and Assessment** specific to a unit. These assessment goals correspond to the levels of reasoning on the Assessment Pyramid. Included are formative and summative assessment items, their location within the text or written assessment, and the level of each item.

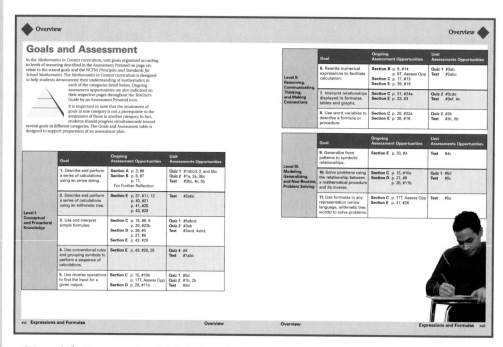

- **Materials Preparation** This helps the teacher to organize materials for the entire unit.

Teachers Matter

For each section of the Student Book, a two-page overview is provided in the Teacher's Guide.

- **Section Focus** describes the mathematical content of the section.
- **Pacing and Planning** delineates daily suggestions for introduction, classwork, and homework
- **Materials** for this specific section includes student and teacher resources
- **Learning Lines** describes the flow of the section mathematically

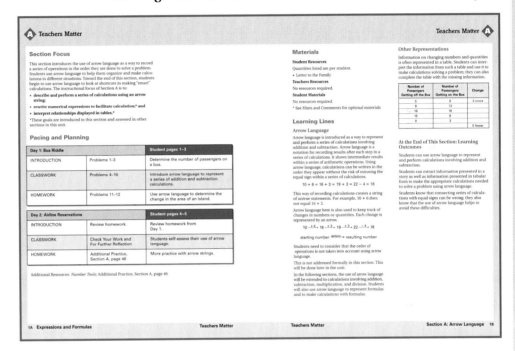

- **Learning Outcomes** helps the teacher to understand what students should know and be able to do at the end of the section.

Teacher's Guide Pages for Instruction

Each Student Book page is reproduced in reduced size on the left page of the Teacher's Guide. In the wrap around the student page, specific teaching tools are included at point of use:

- **Notes** These teaching suggestions were written by experienced MiC teachers and are specific to the problem or context at hand.
- **Assessment Pyramid** This icon identifies problems that can be used for formative assessment. The three layers of the pyramid reflect the three levels of reasoning described on pages xiv and xv of each Teacher's Guide.

Teacher's Guide—Features

- **Reaching All Learners** This section contains alternative approaches for a variety of student needs:

  - **Intervention** provides for students who are having difficulty.

  - **Advanced Learners** offers extension activities for deepening students' understanding.

  - **Writing Opportunity** includes specific writing suggestions associated with the problems.

  - **Extensions** offers additional problems that build from the problems on the page.

  - **Vocabulary Building** highlights words that students need to understand

  - **English Language Learners** suggests strategies for working with students for whom English is a second language.

  - **Parent Involvement** highlights activities with which students can engage their families in mathematical discussions and problem-solving.

  - **Accommodations** offers ideas to address specific student needs.

  - **Hands-On Learning** suggests activities to actively engage students.

- Opposite each student page, **Solutions and Samples** of student work as well as a **Hints and Comments** column are provided. Included in the **Hints and Comments** column on most of the pages are:

  - **Materials** A list of required and optional materials is provided.

  - **Overview** The work students do is briefly described.

  - **About the Mathematics** This section provides background information about the mathematics in the problems and cites other sections and units in which the mathematics is formally introduced or expanded. It offers a quick refresher for teachers about the mathematics.

  - **Planning** Provided here are suggestions for introducing the context or the mathematical concepts; the identification of optional problems and problems that can be used as informal assessment or homework; and suggestions for grouping students—individuals, pairs, small groups, or whole class.

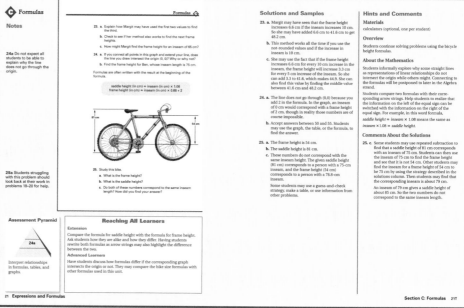

- **Comments About the Solutions** Discussion questions and comments about student strategies, models, and responses are included for selected problems, offering additional insights into student thinking.

- **Technology** Opportunities to use computer applets or other technology to enhance student understanding are located here.

- **Writing Opportunities** Specific suggestions for related writing activities that students may enter in their journals are included.

- **Did You Know?** This section offers historical or other interesting information about the context or the mathematics.

- **Assessment Opportunity** Extra problems that can be used to assess student understanding are included in this section.

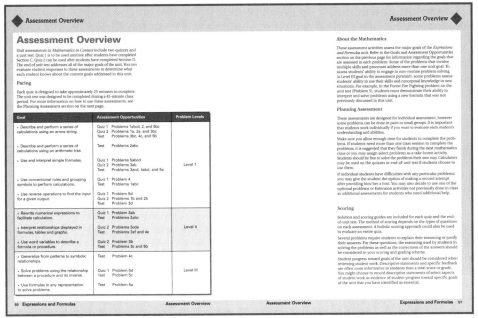

In the Back of the Teacher's Guide

Additional Practice This section contains additional problems and solutions for each section. Additional Practice is also a part of the Student Books.

Assessment Overview correlates the assessment problems of the quizzes and tests with the goals of the unit. The level for each problem is also included. **About the Mathematics**, **Planning Assessment**, and **Scoring** offer additional hints for the teacher to inform assessment.

Unit Assessments include two quizzes (25 minutes each) and a Unit Test (45 minutes). A Solution and Scoring Guide is included for each assessment.

Glossary Definitions of the vocabulary words indicated in the unit appear here. It includes the mathematical terms that are new to students, as well as words having to do with the contexts introduced in the unit. The Glossary is not in the Student Book, so students can construct their own definitions based on their personal understanding of the unit activities.

Blackline Masters Reproducible blackline masters can be found in this section; these include a Letter to the Family introducing the unit's mathematics and **Student Activity Sheets (SAS)** used for selected problems in the Student Book.

Mathematics in the Middle!

What elementary program best leads in to *Mathematics in Context*?

The program or curriculum that is used in elementary schools should have little or no effect on the choice of *Mathematics in Context* for the middle grades. NSF-funded programs at the elementary school may make a transition easier since students will be more accustomed to explaining, justifying, investigating, and strategizing. Regardless of the program used, it is expected that students will have experience with whole number computation and ordering, understand the concept of a fraction as a ratio, recognize basic geometric shapes, understand the decimal number system as it relates to money, and have some experiences with problem solving. These are the only assumptions made for beginning Level 1 in *Mathematics in Context*.

The Algebra Questions

Will students be ready for Algebra 1 in grade 8?

The flexibility of the MiC curriculum allows districts to tailor the program to meet local algebra preparation goals. MiC has a strong focus on algebraic thinking beginning with the Level 1 units. Students develop a deep conceptual understanding of the principles of algebra in Levels 2 and 3 units. Some schools may choose to use MiC Levels 1 and 2 as preparation for algebra in grade 8. Students who successfully complete all three levels of MiC will be well-prepared for algebra in grade 9. Exceptional students who complete two years of MiC will be ready for algebra in grade 8.

Will the students have the equivalent of an Algebra 1 course at the end of Level 3?

This is a more difficult question. There are four Algebra strand units at Level 3; the topics covered include (but are not limited to) linear functions, factoring, exponential functions, recursive and direct formulas, slope, quadratics, sequences, tangent ratio, and so on. Many of these are topics found in Algebra 1. Some topics are even more advanced! However, MiC students have less experience with symbolic manipulation than in a traditional Algebra 1 course. *Algebra Rules!*, one of the new units in the revision, was specifically added to enhance the formalization of algebraic concepts. *Algebra Tools* also provides additional practice with algebraic topics. Districts and schools may need to look at the standards for algebra within their local area to make this decision.

What high school program best follows MiC?

The high school mathematics program selected to follow MiC may be either NSF-funded or traditional. Students completing MiC have been successful using either type of program. They have a strong background in mathematical reasoning, a deep understanding of algebraic thinking, and are confident problem solvers. These qualities usually lead to a successful performance in high school mathematics.

Tides at the Golden Gate Bridge

Implementation of *Mathematics in Context*

Mathematics in Context Pilots

Some districts opt to pilot one or more units from *Mathematics in Context* in the year before purchase. If your district makes this choice, it is important to remember that specific units in MiC have prerequisites and may not be suitable for pilots.

Units to choose: it may be suitable to use a Level 1 unit at either grade 6 or grade 7 and Level 2 units at grade 7 or 8. Level 3 units are usually better to pilot only in grade 8 or at the end of the year in grade 7. Pre-algebra students or gifted and talented classes may be the exception to this rule.

It is also suggested that MiC units be used to replace chapters in the text. Do not try to use a few pages from the unit as this will not really let you and your students experience MiC lessons.

Suggested pilot units:

Grade 6	Grade 7	Grade 8
Picturing Numbers	Reallotment	Revisiting Numbers
Models You Can Count On	Figuring All the Angles	Packages and Polygons
Expressions and Formulas	Facts and Factors	Building Formulas
Take a Chance	Triangles and Beyond	Insights into Data

Descriptions of the mathematical content of these units may be found in the Unit Overviews in the front of this book. Time of the year and district standards may influence your decisions on which units to pilot. Pilot in-services and support from former classroom teachers is available during the time of the pilot.

Implementing *Mathematics in Context*

Just as *Mathematics in Context* does not prescribe a single strategy for students to use in solving a problem, the teacher support materials (including this book) do not prescribe a single way of implementing the curriculum. Different teachers, schools, and districts will have different needs and experiences with mathematics curricula, which will influence implementation decisions. While this *Teacher Implementation Guide* is intended to provide general guidance about how to implement this curriculum, the final decision rests with the classroom teacher.

Preparing for Implementation of MiC

Ideally your school or district has been planning for the implementation of MiC several months (or even years) in advance. The academic year and summer before an implementation are important times to work out some of the decisions related to an effective implementation. Although these decisions vary from district to district, here are some of the common decisions to be made.

Before Implementation

In general, the more collaborative experiences teachers have prior to teaching their first unit the better. Teachers need to experience MiC lessons and learn to navigate through the teacher materials. Pedagogical changes may need to be made, and change is not always easy.

Implementation of MiC depends on a results-driven and comprehensive program of professional development. Many factors impact the amount of professional development that is available for teachers. In-service workshops and training are recommended for effective implementation.

Three-Day Overview Workshop: A workshop of this type consists of four half days focused on the four content strands, a half day on assessment, and a half day preparing the first unit of the year's sequence. A key feature of this workshop is engaging teachers in the activities as if they were students. This allows the presenter to model effective pedagogy and discuss the learning lines and management issues.

Unit-Specific Training: This half-day (minimum) workshop is intended to prepare teachers to teach their next unit. It is usually facilitated by someone who is very familiar with the unit under consideration. Teachers are typically led through the unit section by section. Depending on the time available, teachers work only with the student materials and do the problems as if they were students before they get to use the Teacher's Guide. This allows teachers to experience the different ways students will approach the problems. Teachers are also able to think ahead about manipulatives that will be needed and issues related to classroom assessment.

Strand Overview Workshops: The purpose of this training is to provide teachers with an in-depth look at each of the strands. This workshop involves teachers at each of the three grade levels. It is similar to unit training in that teachers work the problems as if they were students. The difference is that the goal is to understand the structure of the strand and to see how the long learning lines develop over time. In this way, teachers see how the units they teach at their level contribute to the learning line. They also see where the mathematics goes beyond their grade level units. Likewise teachers at the higher grade levels see what experiences and understandings they can expect students to have coming into their grade level. Since this type of training will take several hours, it would probably happen over several after-school study sessions or on a professional development day. The most successful training of this type focuses on tracing themes or sub-strands such as the following from the Algebra strand: Patterns and Regularities, Restrictions, Variables, Representations, and Linearity.

Structured and organized professional development activities offer time for collaboration. However, if an experienced facilitator is not available, two or more teachers can facilitate it on their own. The time spent working together is invaluable. National and Local Users Conferences are also scheduled in various geographic areas throughout the summer.

Additional Preparation before School Starts

Assign teaching responsibilities. If you teach in a team of more than one mathematics teacher, decide within the math-science or other teaching team who will teach each unit. If at all possible, have two or more teachers teach the same unit simultaneously so they can prepare together and periodically discuss their experiences with the unit.

Make a schedule. Identify the days on which you plan to begin each unit and mark them on a calendar. (Be sure the calendar includes non-instructional days such as holidays, field trips, and in-service days.) You'll find the suggested number of days for each section of the unit in the **Pacing and Planning** chart of the Section Overview pages of each Teacher's Guide.

Because of the rich mathematical content of the units, it is easy to spend more time on a unit than you originally planned, so check your schedule every week or so to adjust your target dates if necessary. MiC is a spiral curriculum, and mastery develops over time; do not spend too much time on any one unit.

Review the classroom's physical arrangement. Because interaction among students and between students and the teacher is important, make sure that the arrangement of the classroom is conducive to working in small groups or pairs as well as whole-class discussion.

Develop a materials list. Many of the activities in the units require or can be supported with additional materials, which are listed under **Materials Preparation** on page xviii of each Teacher's Guide. Review the materials lists for items you may need to order or gather.

Preparation for Teaching a Unit

You can begin preparing for each unit by familiarizing yourself with the mathematical content of the unit. Read the Overview in the Teacher's Guide, paying particular attention to the following:

- Math in the Unit on page viii
- The Strand Overview on pages x–xiii
- Goals column of the Goals and Assessment charts on pages xvi and xvii

Also read the Teachers Matter pages, the first of which is on pages 1A and 1B. You may want to preview the Summaries and Check Your Work, which are at the end of each section of the Student Book and Teacher's Guide.

The most important preparation for teaching this curriculum is working through all of the problems in order, as if you were a student. Come up with your own solutions and—if at all possible—discuss them with a colleague who is working through the same unit. After you finish the activities on each page or section of the Student Book, review the facing page(s) in the Teacher's Guide. This page contains Solutions and Samples of student work and Hints and Comments for teaching.

By working through the problems yourself, you can appreciate the alternating struggle and enlightenment that awaits your students. You will gain insight into students' reasoning and common misunderstandings. You may also discover an even broader range of solutions and strategies than could be described in the Teacher's Guides.

Preparation for Substitute Teachers

Substitutes should first read the philosophy of *Mathematics in Context* on page 58. You may want to make a copy of these pages and include them with your plans for substitutes. The length of time the substitute will be teaching and the students' familiarity with the curriculum will determine the specific lesson plan.

When substitutes teach a day or two during the first six weeks of the school year, it may be preferable to use activities from *Number Tools* or *Algebra Tools*. Continuing with activities in the middle of a unit may be too challenging since neither the substitute nor the students are familiar with the mathematical reasoning and discussion that are essential in *Mathematics in Context*.

When the substitute will be teaching for more than a few days, continuing with the unit is necessary. Spending one day on an activity from *Number Tools* or *Algebra Tools* may be a good way for the substitute to become familiar with the curriculum. A long-term substitute can prepare by talking with a teacher who is familiar with *Mathematics in Context*. Reading the Math in the Unit on page viii, and the Strand Overview on pages x–xiii of the Teacher's Guide, as well as the Teachers Matter pages of the Teacher's Guide, is also recommended.

Later in the year, students will have developed the habit of reasoning and discussing their problem-solving strategies, so the substitute should continue teaching the unit. If time permits, the substitute should skim the Math in the Unit on page viii, and the Strand Overview on pages x–xiii of the Teacher's Guide and the relevant Teachers Matter. The focus of the class should remain on communication of the students' understanding and problem-solving strategies. When the regular teacher returns, students can share the responsibility of explaining what they have learned.

Preparation for Mid-Year Transfer Students

In most cases, a few days of gradually increasing participation will sufficiently introduce transfer students to the *Mathematics in Context* curriculum. Pairing the transfer student with another student is also helpful. Because transfer students will not be familiar with the number models used in MiC, sections of *Number Tools* or a few activities from preceding units can be used to develop prerequisite skills and understanding.

Introducing Students to *Mathematics in Context*

The first year that students use *Mathematics in Context*, let them know that it may be very different from the textbooks they have used in the past. Your students may not be accustomed to thinking and communicating about mathematics. In addition, they may not be accustomed to evaluating problem-solving strategies suggested by their classmates. When you introduce *Mathematics in Context* to your students, consider sharing the following ideas:

- *Mathematics in Context* is more than computation. It will encourage teachers and students to think about mathematics in different ways. This curriculum will help students develop thinking and reasoning skills that they can use for the rest of their lives. (Tell students that the drawings and materials they will use to solve problems are also are very different from what they are used to, but they will help to make the mathematics clearer.)

- Most of the problems can be solved and explained in more than one way, and many problems have more than one solution. The goal is to discuss different strategies and then decide whether some work better for particular problems. Explain that sometimes you will ask certain students to share their ideas and at other times you will ask the same students to listen to and analyze other students' ideas.

- To give students more opportunities to explain their thinking and understand someone else's thinking, students will sometimes work in pairs or small groups.

- Explain that students may be surprised by the variety of mathematical topics they will learn about. This variety of topics will give each of them a chance to excel—and to be challenged—regardless of how easy or difficult mathematics has been for them in the past.

Conducting a *Mathematics in Context* Class

The Teacher's Guide makes pacing suggestions for moving through the unit. Many teachers start a class period by getting the students into (or back into) the context. Some teachers like to introduce a new section or context by having one person read aloud.

It is important to assess whether students are familiar with the context or not. For example, students in a small town might not know about a big city subway system, and likewise students in the Midwest might never have experienced tides. A little discussion at the beginning of each new context can help students understand the important ideas of the context so that they can engage in the mathematics. Many teachers verify that students understand the context by engaging the whole class in the initial questions about that context.

After the context is established, students can work on the next few problems on their own or in their groups. This gives the teacher an opportunity to work with individual students and to assess the range of strategies that students are using on the problems. After an appropriate amount of time, it is important that the teacher pull the students back into a whole class discussion of critical problems as a way to share strategies and to make sure misconceptions are identified. It is not necessary to discuss every problem in class. The Hints and Comments in the Teacher's Guide will identify the most important problems for whole class discussion.

Successful implementation of *Mathematics in Context* depends on the teacher's ability to create a climate in which students are willing to risk thinking in new ways and communicating about their discoveries. If the teacher values multiple perspectives, students will be more respectful listeners and more willing to volunteer their ideas. Use directions such as "Listen to this student's explanation. How is it different from yours?" to help students develop listening and critical-thinking skills.

The interaction that is related to a particular topic that occurs on a particular day is important, but students will have additional opportunities to explore that topic. All the important mathematical concepts are revisited many times throughout the curriculum. If for some reason the interaction on one day is not as meaningful as you had hoped, make a note about what you can do differently in the future, and move on. If necessary, you can take a few minutes of the next class to summarize the ideas from the previous day.

Students spend a great deal of class time working on problems during which they either reinvent mathematics or apply concepts they have already learned. They may work individually, in pairs, in small groups, or as a whole class, depending on your preference. Your role during these investigations is to encourage interaction among students.

Have students share their discoveries within their small group or periodically with the whole class. Whole-class discussions are helpful when students have difficulty with a specific problem, when you want students to compare and evaluate various problem-solving strategies, and when you want students to summarize what they have learned.

Encouraging Mathematical Thinking

Sometimes, especially during the first few weeks of school, students may be unsure about how to approach a problem. They may try to persuade you to tell them how to solve the problem or complain that a problem is too hard. Although it can be difficult to watch students struggle, it is often a necessary step in helping them develop the mathematical thinking skills that will allow them to use mathematics effectively. Ideally you will convey to your students that you have high expectations for them, that it is O.K. that they don't know how to do the problem right away, and that you are confident that they can find a solution.

If students are having difficulty with a problem, ask open-ended questions and provide hints. For example, you might ask "What do you know about the problem?" or "What are you asked to find?" Based on students' responses, ask probing questions such as "Since this problem is about comparing, can you think of any ways to make comparisons? Do you think any of these ways might apply to this problem? Could drawing a picture help?"

Orchestrating Mathematical Discussions

Well-orchestrated discussions give students a chance to communicate their ideas and expand their understanding because of the variety of ideas they hear. Discussions also allow students to make connections to their prior learning and to their daily lives. Whenever students work on problems individually or in small groups, walk around the room and try to identify those students who have different approaches. Then call on those students and conduct a discussion to uncover this variety.

Sometimes, depending on the concept and the composition of the class, a whole-class discussion is not necessary. Bringing together two or three small groups or pairs of students may provide sufficient interaction.

Certain strategies are highlighted in the Teacher's Guides as particularly effective. If students do not reinvent these strategies after several minutes of discussion, try asking leading questions. If students still don't suggest these strategies, you can describe these strategies. "Here is another way that students solve this problem." Be careful not to present these other suggestions as the most effective. Allow students to evaluate them just as they evaluate the other strategies presented.

Although students should be encouraged to use any strategy they understand to solve a problem, some strategies are more efficient and generalizable than others. It is a challenge for teachers to value all strategies on the one hand and to move students toward more abstract strategies on the other. Teachers can accomplish this through discussion and student-led evaluation of the strategies. In most cases, students will naturally adopt more sophisticated strategies as they understand them. In some cases, students will need extra encouragement to move on to more efficient strategies. However, students should always be able to go back to more informal strategies when they need to.

Too Little or Too Much Discussion

When discussion is sparse, continue to ask probing questions and allow ample time for students to think of responses. Sometimes a teacher's supportive silence is very effective in sparking a discussion.

You do not have to discuss all strategies that are present in a classroom. When discussions run long, acknowledge that students have identified several ways to approach a problem and that there may be even more but that you need to move on to another problem. Consider suggesting to students that they write their additional ideas in their math notebooks or journals.

Some discussions lead naturally to extension activities that can be assigned as homework in mathematics or other subjects. However, if time permits or if students are very animated about a discussion, you may want to take a few more minutes to explore the topic in greater depth or find additional connections to students' daily lives.

Summarizing and Synthesizing the Discussion

When several strategies have been presented and discussed, the teacher should try to summarize the discussion before moving on. This can be done at the end of the class period: "Today we have seen several strategies. Which one do you like best and why?" Similar questions can also be the basis for a writing assignment at the end of the class period or for homework. Teachers might also start class the next day with these questions.

Teacher's Knowledge of Mathematics

Regardless of your prior knowledge of mathematics, the curriculum will almost certainly challenge you to think in new ways and delight you with its accessible content. At least once during the year, you will be surprised by a student's problem-solving strategy. Be honest about your surprise, and don't pretend to know all the answers. At first, you may feel awkward stepping away from the familiar algorithms to look at the problems from your students' perspectives.

If you are less comfortable about your knowledge of mathematics, you may be concerned about the sophistication and variety of concepts in the curriculum. Familiar problem contexts and informal introductions to concepts make challenging concepts accessible to everyone. Working through the problems yourself with the help of the Teacher's Guide and a colleague, if possible, will usually help you understand the mathematics.

If you don't understand a student's description or explanation during class, ask the student to restate it or support it with drawings or models. Remember one of the goals of the curriculum is for students to use mathematics to communicate effectively. You may also want to ask whether a second student can explain the first student's ideas in a different way.

Grouping Strategies

In a typical classroom, students will work in many different grouping arrangements, depending on the situation. At the beginning and end of each class session, the teacher might want to lead whole class discussions. During seat work it is good to have students talking to other students, so pairs or groups of four are recommended. Groups also work well when students are at different reading levels or when the class contains English language learners. It is common for teachers to switch student groupings several times during a class session. For example, using Think–Pair–Share, students initially work alone (think) on a problem, then compare their solution with someone else (pair), and finally discuss (share) the solutions in a whole class setting. This sequence could be repeated to a series of problems.

Teachers who are not accustomed to having students work in groups sometimes worry that they need special training in group work before they can begin. Such training might be helpful, but it is not necessary. The following guidelines cover many of the questions teachers have about groups.

- Four is a good size for a group. Fewer students might limit the conversation and more might make it difficult for all students to participate.

- Mixed ability groups are recommended. However, monitor so that everyone in the group contributes and that the group is not dominated by the higher ability students.

- Change groups during the school year so that students have a chance to work with other students.

- Consider management issues when assigning groups. Talking is a natural result of group work; disruptive behaviors should be controlled.

Homework: Assigning and Reviewing

There are many different ways to assign homework using MiC.

- The Pacing and Planning chart in the beginning of each section of the Teacher's Guide makes specific suggestions for problems that can be done at home.

- For each section there are Additional Practice problems at the end of the Student Book. These can be assigned a few at a time as the material is taught or all together at the end of the section.

- Pages from *Number Tools* or *Algebra Tools* can be used where appropriate to practice a skill or to introduce a skill that a student might have missed.

Whenever homework is assigned, you will need to decide how to review it the next day. With some of problems, you will need to discuss them in class the next day before you can continue with new material, while with others, you can continue unless students have specific questions.

Managing Softbound Units and Student Notebooks

The softbound units of MiC can be protected from excessive wear by having students put them in three-hole binders. These binders can also hold Student Activity Sheets and spiral notebooks for students to record their work. The notebooks can be collected periodically for checking or grading.

Professional Development

Research indicates that effective implementation of *Mathematics in Context* (MiC) relies on a results-driven and comprehensive professional development program. Holt, Rinehart and Winston will work with you to deliver professional services unparalleled in education, customized and planned to positively impact instruction.

Mathematics in Context workshops and services are designed specifically to support the initial, ongoing, and expanded implementation of *Mathematics in Context*. Each workshop is designed to meet the needs of teachers, mathematics learners, supervisors, administrators, and parents of children using *Mathematics in Context*. The workshops reflect the latest in professional development research and adult-learning theory and are delivered by consultants from the *Mathematics in Context* development team from the University of Wisconsin as well as experienced, certified *Mathematics in Context* specialists.

Local and National Users' Conferences and Leadership Conferences for Mathematics in Context are scheduled each summer. Information on all scheduled MiC events may be found at www.hrw.com Professional Development.

The comprehensive package of in-service options offered are listed on the following page. Selection of workshops and services is dependent on the needs of your local district or school and the results you wish to achieve.

Professional Development Menu of Services

Product Orientation

Each 1- to 3-hour session is designed to meet the needs of a particular segment of the learning community. Each session will include a complete description of the MiC curriculum and its components, specific action items for each group, and engaging and lively discussions aimed at easing the implementation of the program.

MiC PO1 Teacher Orientation

MiC PO2 Administrator Orientation

MiC PO3 Parent Orientation

MiC PO4 Summer School Orientation

Content Workshops

Each 3- to 6-hour session is designed to foster the development of the MiC educator as a teacher and learner of mathematics. Consultants model instructional strategies as teachers experience lessons from the curriculum. Pedagogy, mathematical content, connections within and among strands, assessment, class management, and planning are integral to each training session.

MiC CW1 New User Grade Level Unit Training

MiC CW2 New User Teacher Leader Training

MiC CW3 Experienced User Grade Level Training

MiC CW4 Experienced User Teacher Leader Training

MiC CW5 Cross-Grade Strand Development

Specialized Workshops

Typically 3 to 6 hours in length, these workshops are tailored to the needs of districts and designed to align to state and local standards. Special arrangements for these workshops should be made through the Professional Development Office.

MiC SW1 Meeting the Needs of Special Education Students

MiC SW2 Classroom Coaching

MiC SW3 On-site Demonstration Lessons and Co-teaching

MiC SW4 Assessment in MiC

MiC SW5 Keynote Address

Consultation and Planning Services
(Value based on time and personnel requirement)

A consultant from our Professional Development Planning Team will work with the district to plan, design, and implement professional development. Written correlations and lesson planning and document design fall within the scope of these services.

MiC CP1 Initial Planning

MiC CP2 Comprehensive Consultation and Planning

MiC CP3 Local Correlation and Design

Special Projects

Districts may have needs that are not covered in our Menu of Services. Special Projects may be approved if they are cost efficient and within the scope of our specialists.

Working with Families

Families may have questions and concerns about *Mathematics in Context*. It is suggested that a Parent's Night be held before school begins to address the concerns and to convince families that student learning is supported by research.

Questions and suggested responses follow.

Why is my child struggling more than before?

The transition to MiC can challenge what it means to do well in mathematics. Students who produced accurate, fast answers to computation problems in a traditional classroom might experience difficulty when they are expected to justify, explain, and reason mathematically. Likewise, students who struggled with arithmetic might begin to shine when multiple strategies are available to solve problems, and conceptual understanding is valued.

Teachers can help parents and students understand that mathematics isn't necessarily about speed and memorization—that being able to grapple with a problem, trying various approaches, and finally reaching an accurate answer are also important. Teachers can reduce everyone's frustrations by communicating with students and their parents the idea that spending concentrated time on a problem is a part of the learning process.

Why doesn't the book offer an explanation of how to do the homework? I don't know how to help my child.

Suggest that family members encourage their children to talk about mathematics outside of school. The Letter to the Family, which is a blackline master in the Teacher's Guide, identifies mathematical situations in daily life. Asking general questions about a student's work is a technique that family members can use even when they may not fully understand the mathematics in a problem. For example, they might ask, *Can you explain how you solved this problem? Are there other ways to solve this problem? Are there other solutions? Why did you choose this way or this solution?*

To help a student with homework, family members can use a similar strategy. They can ask questions such as *What do you know about this problem? What do you know that might be related to this problem? Can you understand the problem better if you make a drawing or model? What have you done so far to solve the problem?* Explain that sometimes just getting students to articulate what they know or have done is enough to help them move forward.

The answers to Check Your Work problems are provided in the back of the Student Books. This is a place for parents to see solutions and help their child find a solution. Suggest to families that they review each section with their child and have the child explain how they reached the solution.

Why won't the teacher answer students' questions?

Parents often have a limited notion of what constitutes "teaching." Their own experiences as students lead them to think that teaching is telling. So if a teacher does not tell students how to do something, misunderstandings can arise. Teachers should share with parents and students why they are sometimes unwilling to answer questions. Teachers will often try to have questions answered by other group members in order to foster discussion and to encourage group ownership of the results.

Where is the math?

Along with a narrow definition of teaching, parents often have a narrow definition of what constitutes mathematics. They might not recognize the math they will encounter in the units. Explain that the curriculum actually has rich mathematics in a realistic context. Although *Mathematics in Context* doesn't have recognizable computation problems, every unit is full of problems that require students to use computation, estimation, and a variety of other mathematics. Invite families to experience the math firsthand by working through a page or two from the first section of a unit. They can do the work at an Open House or at home with their children.

A few families might need more information about the mathematics in the curriculum. Consider giving them a copy of the Goals and Assessment charts on pages xvi and xvii of a Teacher's Guide and mentioning that these are one-ninth of the year's goals. Draw their attention to the first section of the chart, Conceptual and Procedural Knowledge. Tell them that most programs include only these kinds of goals, but as they can see from the other two parts of the chart, *Mathematics in Context* also emphasizes a deeper understanding of mathematics.

Why is there so much reading and writing?

In MiC students are often expected to respond to questions with written explanations to demonstrate their understanding of the mathematics. Teachers can share with parents the strategies they use to accommodate the range of reading and writing skills found in a typical class. Engaging in a mathematics curriculum that is reading and writing intensive is likely to improve a student's reading comprehension and writing clarity along with their mathematical understanding. Many state assessments require this degree of reading, writing, justifying, and explaining.

Is there any evidence that the MiC approach is effective?

Refer parents to the MiC website for research data. Or give them a copy of the Summary Report (available from Holt, Rinehart and Winston). Let them see and read about student success.

Is my child learning basic skills?

Parents need to see that skill development is embedded in investigations rather than in long sets of out-of-context practice problems. MiC engages students in mathematically rich contexts where students *encounter and use* number operations even as they are learning topics in data analysis, algebra, and geometry. To help with parent concerns about basic skills, make sure that some of the homework focuses on skill building and involve parents in the refinement of those skills.

Parents are also looking for reassurance about the use of calculators. Communicate that calculators and computers are used as tools in appropriate situations, as are mental math, estimation, and paper-and-pencil algorithms. Knowing which tool is appropriate for a given task is something for both parents and students to learn. This is a good topic for back-to-school night. Parents can be given a variety of specific examples of tasks that would call for different methods of computation. When parents know the expectations of their child's teacher, they can reinforce them at home.

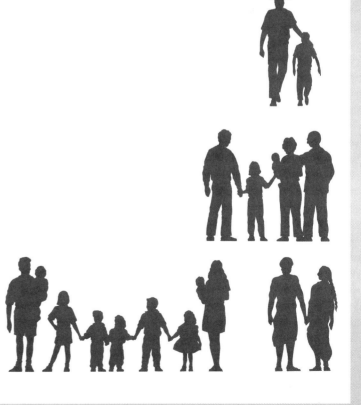

Reaching All Students

One of the guiding principles of MiC is that mathematics is a subject—and a way of thinking—that all students can learn. This principle is evidenced in the use of models, in the contexts that make sense to students, and in the valuing and encouragement of multiple solution strategies. However, not all students come to MiC with the same ability to learn mathematics. Some students will need more support for their learning.

In the Reaching All Learners box on the Teacher's Guide page, MiC offers suggestions to make the mathematics accessible and appropriate for students with different learning styles, abilities, and disabilities. The goal of these adaptations is to provide access to the math concepts and skills in the lesson in order to meet the needs of diverse learners and thereby increase their chances of success. Although these suggestions cover the most common accommodations, teachers will sometimes need to redesign and adjust the materials to meet the needs of specific learners.

The following suggestions for reaching all learners are based upon the National Science Foundation supported project *Addressing Accessibility in Middle School Mathematics* at the Educational Development Corporation.

Guiding Assumptions

- All students can learn mathematics if given proper support.
- All students fall on a continuum of learner differences. Students with disabilities are part of that continuum, rather than a separate category.
- Adapting curriculum and instruction is appropriate for all learners, not just students with disabilities.
- Making adaptations is a collaborative process that involves general and special educators.
- Teachers are responsible for the success of all their students.

Accessibility Strategies

The *Addressing Accessibility* project identifies three categories of strategies for making mathematics accessible to all students: General Instructional, Curriculum Adaptation, and Classroom Environment. A few examples of strategies in each category are given below.

General Instructional Strategies:
- Provide both visual and auditory directions
- Set up a notebook organizational system
- Read aloud
- Offer manipulatives

Curriculum Adaptation Strategies:
- Adjust the level of difficulty by the use of friendlier numbers, simple language, or reduce the complexity of the task
- Change the context to make it more familiar
- Provide templates for tables, graphs, writing, and other tasks

Classroom Environment Strategies:
- Post homework assignments in a consistent location
- Display wall charts with key vocabulary and information
- Have graph paper, templates available

It is clear that many of these suggestions benefit all students, while others apply to some students with very specific needs.

Accommodations

Teachers often need to make adaptations to the MiC curriculum materials to address the specific needs of students. The chart below shows categories of student needs followed by a sampling of specific tasks and student needs within those categories and a possible accessibility strategy to address that particular need.

Category of Need	Specific Task	Student Need	Possible Accessibility Strategy
Conceptual	Make generalizations	Finds it difficult to make generalizations and to write rules	Provide rules for the student to test
Language	Follow verbal directions	Has difficulty with auditory processing of verbal information	Provide written as well as oral directions
Visual-Spatial Processing	Read handouts and book pages	Finds crowded pages distracting	Reorganize material into a single-sided handout
Organization	Collect and record data	Records data in a disorganized manner that is difficult to analyze	Use table templates for data collection
Memory	Solve multi-step problems	Does not have needed information in working memory to solve a problem	Break problem into smaller chunks
Attention	Participate in class discussions	Distracts the group	Break into small groups and have them report back to large groups
Psycho-Social	Move through a frustration point	Gets frustrated easily	Check to make sure students have the necessary prerequisites

Assessment for Special Learners

The leveled assessments provided with MiC make it easy to differentiate assessment and to write educational plans for students. Formative assessment items indicated by the Assessment Pyramid on the teacher pages let you check student progress through the lessons. Success on Level 1 summative assessment problems may be a goal for only some students. Do allow these students to try all items, but be cognizant of the fact that only some students may be successful on the Level 3 items.

The Test and Practice Generator allows teachers to provide more space for answers, change the font size for visually impaired learners, decrease the number of items on a test, decrease the number of items in a multiple-choice answer, change the scales on graphs, use friendlier numbers for problems: many choices and many ways to accommodate the needs of special learners.

Cautions

There are a few cautions to consider.

- Do not intervene too soon. Expect students to succeed. Unless there is an obvious need for intervention (for example, enlarging a worksheet for a student with a visual impairment), give students a chance to work the problems on their own as written. Student satisfaction follows some struggle with a problem, but do not let the frustration level get too high.

- Do not lose the integrity of the mathematics. Teachers need to know the goals of the lesson and the entire unit. Some concepts are required for all students; do not eliminate these vital topics for any students. Professional development and planning with other teachers can help in identifying the critical mathematics.

- Do not reduce the mathematics to skill sets. In an effort to help students who struggle, it is common for teachers to intervene and reduce the problem to a set of procedures to be followed with the result that they take away all the thinking. Understanding the concept is important to learning and retention of concepts.

- Do not eliminate the investigative nature of the mathematics. Remember that a goal of MiC is that students be able to mathematize their world. This requires investigation, conjecture, discussion, and justification. Try not to scaffold the problems so deeply that no investigation is required.

Working with Advanced Students

Special learners include those who are very talented in mathematics. The Reaching all Learners boxes in the Teacher's Guide will often make suggestions for ways to extend the lesson through additional challenging questions, problems, or investigations. Innovative ideas for challenging these students are also suggested in the Hints and Comments section of the Teacher's Guides. Teachers may find that students want to move ahead and go directly to formalization. This is clearly suitable for some students; do not insist that they do every problem or use only informal strategies. Make use of the Level 3 assessments that are embedded within the lessons. Use the special projects and enhancement activities. *Number Tools* and *Algebra Tools* also offer some challenging problems; ask students to try to design similar problems or to prove their generalizations.

The curriculum design allows students to progress at their own level of understanding. Progressive formalization, moving from informal to preformal to formal, occurs at different rates for different students; the curriculum design supports all student learning.

The Role of the School Administrator

Support from administrators is a key element in the success of MiC implementations. The following suggestions are some information that MiC developers have learned from teachers and districts who have implemented MiC successfully in the past.

Schedule a Parent's Night

MiC represents a significant change for most parents. They will need an opportunity to learn about MiC and what they can expect their child to experience in a MiC classroom. An evening parent's meeting devoted to MiC is a good way to accomplish this.

- Be positive about the new curriculum. Encourage teachers to also be positive.
- Involve the teachers in activities for parents.
- Engage the parents in doing some math so that they can see how MiC is engaging for students. Choose an activity or lesson that insures parental success.
- Invite someone from outside your district who is knowledgeable about MiC to respond to questions the parents might have.
- Have copies of research on student learning using MiC. (Summary Report of Student Achievement in MiC)

Schedule Planning Time

Teachers new to MiC will need time to meet with other teachers to discuss new units, to plan lessons, and to work out solutions to difficulties that arise. This ongoing communication is facilitated by scheduling common planning periods or monthly meetings devoted to MiC. Whenever possible, administrators should attend these meetings It is important that administrators keep informed on progress and teacher concerns.

Protect Teachers

Implementing a new curriculum like *Mathematics in Context* places demands on teachers. They often need to learn new mathematics, new instructional strategies, and new methods of assessment.

Administrators who recognize these demands will work to protect their teachers from additional demands from outside pressures, such as concerned parents and school board members. The key is to make sure teachers do not need to justify their instructional model or the curriculum that they are using.

Alfie Kohn put it best when he wrote about the pressures resulting from external tests. His words could also apply to curriculum implementation:

> "Finally, whatever your position on the food chain of American education, one of your primary obligations is to be a buffer—to absorb as much pressure as possible from those above you without passing it on to those below. If you are a **superintendent** and must face school board members who want to see higher test scores, the most constructive thing you can do is to protect principals from these ill-conceived demands—to the best of your ability and without losing your job in the process. If you are a **building administrator**, on the receiving end of test-related missives from the central office, your challenge is to shield teachers from this pressure—and, indeed, to help them pursue meaningful learning in their classrooms. If you are a **teacher** unlucky enough to work for an administrator who hasn't read this paragraph, your job is to minimize the impact on students. Try to educate those above you whenever it seems possible to do so, but cushion those below you every day. Otherwise you become a part of the problem."

(Kohn, A. January, 2001, "Fighting the Tests," *Phi Delta Kappan*, p. 351)

Field Parent Concerns

Not all parent concerns will be addressed by a Parent's Night; some of them will only surface as the year progresses. It is important to monitor these concerns in order to provide the appropriate response. Some administrators find it helpful to keep a log of calls received from concerned parents.

Typically concerns can be classified in the following five levels of increasing seriousness:

1. **Concerns of parents who support the program.** A parent wanting to know how they can help their child with homework is an example of this level of concern. A failure to respond to these concerns can lead to the loss of these parents' support.

2. **Concerns resulting from misinformation or no information.** A parent who is worried about the lack of drill and practice in MiC might not understand the spiraling of the curriculum and the embedding of computation within problem solving situations.

3. **Concerns about program implementation.** It takes time for teachers to adjust to the new pedagogy of MiC. They will make mistakes in the first year of implementation. Continued attention on professional development will address these concerns.

4. **Concerns based on lack of trust.** Some parents are uncomfortable with any change, and they lack trust in both MiC and the teachers' ability to use it effectively to educate their child. Administrators can address these concerns with evidence of the district commitment to the implementation.

5. **Concerns based on traditional beliefs about schooling.** Some parents' beliefs about schooling and mathematics will be in conflict with the goals and approach of MiC. Concerns at this level are the hardest to address, because nothing will change their minds. The best response is to seek a compromise for their child.

Support Implementation

Since MiC expects changes in both the mathematics content that is taught and in the way that content is taught, one can expect considerable variation in how the materials are implemented in classrooms by teachers. Fidelity to the content and pedagogy of MiC is a serious issue.

1. To implement MiC well, teachers need training and support. The training needs to be both prior to and during implementation. The support needs to include both administrative assistance and the opportunity for teachers to meet and share on a regular basis (see above on Scheduling Planning Time). Lack of adequate support and in particular isolation of teachers as they teach MiC, lead to poor implementation.

2. The mathematical background and content knowledge of teachers vary. Provide activities and professional development workshops that focus on content for the teacher.

3. Recognize the differences in classroom techniques. MiC focuses on teaching for understanding. This often involves posing contextual problems and having students investigate ways of representing and solving the problems. Do not expect teachers to adhere to a model of teaching that does not support the instructional goals of MiC.

4. Assessments must inform instruction. MiC expects teachers to judge the strategies and quality of answers students provide to complex tasks. Require teachers to use assessments provided with the curriculum. Provide scoring workshops and have teachers share their strategies for evaluating student learning.

5. Understand that talking is a part of the curriculum; interaction between students is to be expected. Straight rows and quiet classes may not indicate success!

Expectations about Student Performance

Student performance as a consequence of implementing MiC depends on answers to three questions.

1. Have the students had an opportunity to learn the content and processes emphasized in MiC?

2. Were the students adequately prepared to study the content of MiC?

3. Is the district's method of assessing student performance aligned with the new curriculum?

Student learning is the central guiding principle for the design of the MiC curriculum. Students master concepts over time; research shows that student scores on assessments will also rise over time. Administrators who recognize these issues will not look for instant results and will instead reserve judgment until the end of the second or third year of implementation.

The MiC Classroom

Building administrators are often responsible for doing periodic observations of teachers' lessons during the school year. What should an administrator look for in a *Mathematics in Context* classroom?

Use of MiC materials:

• The teacher is using MiC units.

• The teacher monitors groups and uses informal assessments.

• There is evidence that the teacher has worked through the problems and understands the mathematical tasks.

Student engagement and communication:

• Students are engaged in complex, higher level problem solving.

• Students collaborate on strategies and solutions.

• Students listen to other students' strategies.

• Students constantly assess their own and others' strategies.

• Students write and explain orally their solutions.

Teacher as facilitator:

• The presentation of the lesson emphasizes conceptual understanding.

• The teacher encourages multiple paths to a solution.

• Discourse between students and teacher includes connections and generalizations (when appropriate).

• The teacher encourages active participation of all students.

• The teacher provides ongoing, purposeful feedback to students to help them make sense of the mathematics and the solutions.

• The teacher asks questions on articulation of thinking, understanding mathematics, or the reasonableness of solutions.

• Mathematical talk time is shared by students and the teacher.

• The teacher exhibits high expectations for all students.

• Students work independently and without constant input from the teacher.

Frequently Asked Questions about MiC

Teacher Professional Development

I am going to teach MiC for the first time. How do I get started?

The best way to get started is to experience the curriculum! Work through a complete unit as though you were a student; do each problem and think about the strategies a student might use. Check the answers and teacher notes and hints in the Teacher's Guide. Note assessments and reflections for each section. This is the best way to get a feel for how MiC develops the mathematical concepts. It also lets you anticipate how students might answer the questions. If you can arrange to do the problems with someone else who is teaching the same unit, you will really have the MiC experience!

How is MiC different from other middle grades textbook series?

When you open an MiC unit, the first thing you will probably see is more text and fewer problems than in a traditional textbook. These words are important because they establish the context, pose questions to the student reader, and summarize important concepts. (See FAQ below for tips on dealing with reading difficulties.) Another difference is that almost all MiC problems are *in context* (not surprising, given the name of the curriculum!). You will rarely see what we call "naked" problems, that is, pages of procedural problems without context. Another difference is that there are usually multiple strategies students will use to solve problems rather than a single algorithm outlined by the text. Student strategies will vary in efficiency, sophistication, and formalism, but they should be valued as long as they are mathematically sound and the student understands what he or she is doing. We expect that over time students will progress to using the more efficient and formal strategies but hopefully not at the expense of understanding.

What professional development is recommended for MiC?

Professional development is critical to the success of implementing MiC. Initially, a complete overview of the curriculum and the resources for the teacher provide structure for implementation. It is suggested that a minimum of six hours be devoted to initial training. It is essential that teachers be comfortable with the first unit they are going to teach. Sustained professional development insures successful implementation. At least quarterly, one full-day workshop for unit training is suggested. A support network either from common planning time or extra time meetings provides immediate feedback and increases the comfort level for each teacher. Continuing professional development activities should include Strand Overviews and also more in depth training on the units. See Professional Development Workshops on page 77.

Are there any general guidelines for teaching with MiC?

Just as we expect students to solve problems using a variety of strategies, so do we expect that there are many different ways to teach MiC effectively. There are, however, specific student expectations in the classroom that are likely to lead to increases in student understanding.

- Students are given the opportunity to talk and work together to solve problems.
- Students are encouraged to explain their thinking and to justify their answers.
- Students are engaged in complex, higher level problem solving.
- Students collaborate on strategies and solutions.
- Students listen to other students' strategies.
- Students constantly assess their own and others' strategies.

What can I use to supplement MiC?

MiC is a complete curriculum that can stand on its own without teachers having to supplement. In those cases where teachers feel additional practice is needed, Additional Practice exercises are provided in the back of the Student Book. Extra practice worksheets may be generated from the Test and Practice Generator or downloaded from MiC Online. *Number Tools* and *Algebra Tools* student workbooks provide practice for the Number strand and Algebra strand units. The Teacher's Guides offer suggestions for enrichment and remediation when necessary.

Do my students have to work in groups all the time?

MiC requires discourse; student to student and student to teacher. A cooperative classroom and an atmosphere that supports different strategies is essential. Students may need time to think about the solutions before sharing strategies. Teachers make decisions about the best groupings for their classrooms; the Teacher's Guides make suggestions regarding grouping for specific problems.

Should I let students take the units home?

MiC units are textbooks. The student units are conveniently three-hole punched for ease of use in a binder. This protects the units and makes it easy for the students to carry all math materials in one binder. The units are used for approximately four weeks, so durability should not be a problem. Usually, parents/guardians want to see the text at home so that they can monitor their student's progress.

What can I do if I don't understand the math in the unit?

What to do? First of all don't panic or otherwise feel bad about yourself. Think of it as an opportunity to learn something new. The next step is to read and study the information in the Teacher's Guide. If it is a particular problem you don't understand, compare your answer to what is in the Teacher's Guide. Maybe you can figure it out from looking at the answers. If the whole topic is unfamiliar to you, use the Math in the Unit section on pages viii and ix and the Section Overviews in the Teacher's Guide. Another strategy is to talk to other MiC teachers in your building, and don't be embarrassed to ask for help. If a student doesn't understand something, we encourage them to ask questions. The same holds true of teachers.

Is it O.K. to use only some pages from a unit and skip the rest?

This is usually not a good idea.

Can I combine MiC with a traditional textbook?

There are specific plans available for combining MiC units with *Holt Middle School Math*. MiC units are used as replacement units, supplementary units, or as a primary curriculum with homework and additional instruction provided in *Holt Middle School Math*. Regardless of the text you are using, MiC may be used to supplement the text or to replace chapters.

Student Learning

How can students learn their math facts without drill and practice?

Students can learn their math facts by application within the problem situations encountered in MiC. Additional practice is not necessary but may be the choice of some teachers.

How can I help students who have reading problems?

Teachers new to MiC are often concerned about the reading demands of MiC for their less able readers. While these concerns are reasonable, one should remember that you don't learn to read by avoiding it. In MiC, students read in order to extract important information, that is they have to read for understanding. However, the words they have to read are about familiar contexts, and they are often accompanied by pictures that support the meaning of the words. Some students need more support. Teachers support students with reading difficulties in a variety of ways. Some teachers read aloud to the class especially when new contexts are introduced. This allows the teacher to make sure that everyone understands new vocabulary and is familiar enough with the context so as to engage in the questions related to it. Another strategy is to group students so that there is always an able reader available.

How can I support English Language Learners using MiC?

The strategies to support ELL students are similar to those for struggling readers with a few additions. Be careful to provide a good balance of the auditory and visual (words and pictures) in your presentations. If there is too much "teacher talk," students with a limited listening vocabulary will soon be lost. If they can see words or representations at the same time, they are more likely to understand. Pairing students to help one another is another useful strategy.

FAQ

How can I adapt MiC for students with learning disabilities?

Before you make any adaptations for learning disabilities, take some time to see how your students do with MiC lessons. Because there are usually several different ways for students to solve problems, students with learning disabilities often have access to the mathematics without adaptations. However, if adaptations are needed, look for suggestions in the Reaching All Learners sections in the Teacher's Guide. Also look on page 80 of the Teacher Implementation Guide for other suggestions.

How does MiC support advanced learners?

Advanced learners are supported by MiC in a number of ways. Sometimes schools accelerate them through the curriculum or a subset of it in order to have them take Algebra I in grade 8 or even earlier. Other times these students are grouped together and allowed to progress through the units at their own rate. If you choose this approach, make sure that students check in with you on a regular basis and that you monitor the quality and depth of their explanations since you will have less chance to hear their discussions and justifications. Another way to work with advanced students is to keep them working with the rest of the class, but to expect more from them in terms of their work. For example, in the Reaching All Learners sections, you will often find ways to extend the lessons or to offer extra challenges.

What should I do if students still don't know the material at the end of a unit?

One of the things that is different about MiC is the notion of mastery. We do not expect students to have mastered most skills and concepts by the end of a single unit. Skills and concepts are often introduced in one unit at an informal level, revisited and deepened in a later unit, and finally formalized and mastered in Level 3 units. So at the end of a unit, teachers should be realistic about the goals of the unit when judging whether or not their students "know the material." The Math in the Unit overview on pages viii and ix in the Teacher's Guide will help you understand the level of understanding expected by the end of the unit. The quizzes and Unit Test provided in the Teacher's Guide of each unit are well aligned with the goals of the unit. If students are successful with these assessments, then they know the material. If they are not successful, then you will remediate as you would with any curriculum. Has the student missed school? Are they attentive and engaged or have they missed something important because of inattention? What specific concept or skill is not understood? To remediate you might assign additional work from the Additional Practice pages from either the end of the Teacher's Guide or appropriate pages in *Number Tools*. Remember that the choice to move to the next unit is often the best decision you can make. A new unit provides a fresh start. You can be sure that concepts and skills will always reappear in another unit, and students will have new opportunities to deepen their understanding.

Resources

Where can I find help planning lessons?

In each Section Overview of the Teacher's Guide, you will find a suggested pacing guide including problems to be used for introduction, class work and homework. The Math in the Unit pages viii and ix will help you understand how these problems fit into the unit and the larger curriculum. After doing these problems yourself, without looking at the answers, you will have a good idea of how students are likely to respond, and you will be able to tailor you planning accordingly. Remember, the goal of planning is not to avoid mistakes by students, but rather to know how to turn them into deeper understanding. And finally, don't forget to talk to other teachers when you are planning.

What manipulatives will I need to do MiC?

Most of the manipulatives you will need for MiC are things that you probably already have in your classroom such as: rulers (centimeters and inches), yard and meter sticks, scissors, graph paper, and tape. Compass cards are used in some units, but they can be made using transparencies and a blackline master found in the Teacher's Guide of *Figuring All the Angles*. The full list of materials needed for each unit can be found in the Teacher's Guide Unit Overview on page xviii. A class set of manipulatives for MiC is also available for the convenience of the teacher.

Technology

Do students need a calculator in sixth grade?

Scientific calculators should be available for all levels of MiC. Some Level 3 units have optional activities involving graphing calculators. There will be times when teachers will not want student to use calculators, for example, when teaching a number unit. When thinking about calculators, a good question to ask is, "Will arithmetic get in the way of students doing significant problem solving?" If the answer is yes, then making calculators available will allow more students access to the mathematics.

What calculator do you recommend?

Most scientific calculators will be appropriate for grades 6 and 7. Look for ones that contain trig functions, square and square roots, a memory key, and that use the standard order of operations. Almost any calculator designed for use in the middle grades is appropriate.

When do students need a graphing calculator with MiC?

Some of the Level 3 units contain optional graphing calculator activities. Graphing calculators are not required in any MiC unit, although using them might enhance student understanding of some topics.

Is there software that goes along with MiC?

Several MiC units make use of applets, which are small programs dedicated to specific tasks. These applets are available via the Internet, and they can be used either in school or at home. The Teacher's Guides identify the applets and where they can be found.

Are computers needed in class?

In general, computers are not needed in class. Sometimes it might be helpful to have one available for demonstration purposes, but they are not required.

Assessment

How can I prepare my students for the end-of-unit assessment?

If students are successful answering the questions posed in the sections, then they will require no additional preparation to be successful on the end-of-unit assessment. Do make sure that students understand how to answer an open response item. Modeling good answers and sharing scoring strategies may be helpful.

Where can I find more assessment problems?

The Test and Practice Generator contains many appropriate MiC problems to allow you to design customized assessments for your students. This collection of problems is searchable by content, problem level (based upon the Assessment Pyramid), and type (open ended, short answer). Many teachers also write their own problems based upon the content of the unit.

How can I be sure my students are learning what they need to learn?

There are a couple of levels to this question. If the question refers to making sure the students have mastered the goals of a particular unit, then read the response to the question above: "*What should I do if students still don't know the material at the end of a unit?*" If the question refers to much bigger issues such as "Are these the right mathematical topics for middle school students to be learning?" or "Will my students be well prepared for high school mathematics?", then one needs to examine the development process that resulted in MiC. Because there is not enough time to teach everything, all curricula involve choices. The choices made for MiC were based upon the philosophy of Realistic Mathematics Education (see page 56 for a fuller discussion of RME), and they are consistent with the recommendations of the NCTM Principles and Standards for School Mathematics. MiC was extensively tested in classrooms, and it has been revised based upon feedback from experienced teachers and extensive review by mathematicians and mathematics educators. Research has shown that if MiC is well implemented, students learn significant mathematics, and they are well prepared to learn mathematics at the high school level.

Parents

What suggestions can I make if parents want to help their children with math homework?

Most teachers are thrilled if parents want to be involved in helping with their child's homework. However, a few guidelines will help.

- The strategies students use on problems might be unfamiliar to parents. Rather than showing their child "the right" way to do the problem, they should ask their child to explain their thinking.

- If a child (and parent) has worked hard on a problem without success, he or she should stop after a reasonable amount of time and ask for help in class the next day.

- If the parent is unfamiliar with the mathematics, he or she can still help by asking questions that will stimulate thought, such as:

  - "Have you done any problems like this before?"

  - "Can you explain what you do understand about this problem?"

  - "What do you think the problem is asking you to do?"

What should be included in a Parents' Night presentation?

Parents' Night is a good way to inform families about MiC. Planners should keep in mind the following points:

- The evening should be introduced by an administrator to provide information on how MiC was selected and to underscore the importance of the implementation effort.

- Parents should engage in activities from MiC. These can be facilitated by teachers who are comfortable with the activity.

- The activities should show significant mathematics that can be approached using different strategies, but should also be easy for the parents to complete.

- Conclude with questions and answers. This part of the evening should be moderated by an administrator. Be prepared for challenging parents. Invite them to set up a later appointment to discuss their concerns.

- Plan for at least one hour but no more than two hours.

Selected *Mathematics in Context* Readings

Bay, J. M. and M. R. Meyer. (March 2003). "What Parents Want to Know About Standards-Based Mathematics Curricula," *Principal Leadership*, National Association of Secondary School Principals, Reston, VA.

Brinker, L. (December 1998). "Using recipes and ratio tables to build on student's understanding of fractions." *Teaching Children Mathematics*, 218–224.

Burrill, G. (December 1998). "Changes in your classroom: From the past to the present to the future." *Mathematics Teaching in the Middle School*, 4(3), 184–190.

Frykholm, J. A. and M. R. Meyer. (May, 2002). "Integrated instruction: Is it science? Is it mathematics?" *Mathematics Teaching in the Middle School*, 7(9), 502–508.

Her, T. and D. C. Webb. (2004). "Retracing a path to assessing for understanding." In T. A. Romberg (Ed.) *Standards-Based Mathematics Assessment in Middle School*. Teachers College Press, Columbia University. NY, 200–220.

Kent, L. B. (September 2000). "Connecting integers to meaningful contexts," *Mathematics Teaching in the Middle School*, 6(1), 62–66.

Meyer, M. R. (August 2004). "New tricks for old dogs." *Mathematics Teaching in the Middle School*, 10(1), 6–7.

Meyer, M. R. (2001). Combination charts representation of linear relationships. In M. S. Smith, G. W. Blume, and M. K. Heid (Co-Eds.) *The Role of Representation in the Teaching and Learning of Mathematics*, Part I. Pennsylvania Council of Teachers of Mathematics, 2001 Yearbook, P. 1–12.

Meyer, M. R. (2001). Representation in Realistic Mathematics Education. In A. Cuoco and F. Curcio (Eds.) *The Roles of Representation in School Mathematics*, Reston, VA: National Council of Teachers of Mathematics, 2001.

Meyer, M. R. (May 1999). "Multiple strategies = multiple challenges." *Mathematics Teaching in the Middle School*, 4(8), 519–523.

Meyer, M. R. (February, 1997). "*Mathematics in context*: Opening the gates to mathematics for all." *NASSP Bulletin*, 53–59.

Meyer, M. R., T. Dekker, and N. Querelle. (May, 2001) "Context in Mathematics Curricula." *Mathematics Teaching in the Middle School*, 6(9), 522–527.

Meyer, M. R. and G. Diopoulos. (September 2002). "Anchored Learning in Context." *Mathematics Teaching in the Middle School*.

Meyer, M. R. and M. A. Ludwig. (January 1999). "Teaching mathematics with MiC: An opportunity for change." *Mathematics Teaching in the Middle School*, 4(4), 264–269.

Meyer, M. R., M. L. Delagardelle, and J. A. Middleton. (April 1996). "Addressing parents' concerns over reform." *Educational Leadership*, 54–57.

Middleton, J. A. and M. van den Heuve-Panhuizen. (1995). "The ratio table." *Mathematics Teaching in the Middle School*, 1(4), 282–288.

Middleton, J. A., M. van den Heuvel-Panhuizen, and J. A. Shew. (1998). "Using bar representations as a model for connecting concepts of rational number." *Mathematics Teaching in the Middle School*, 3(4), 302–312.

Stevens, B. A. (November 2001). "My involvement in change." *Mathematics Teaching in the Middle School*, 7(3), 178–182.

van Reeuwijk, M. and M. Wijers. (1997). "Students' construction of formulas in context." *Mathematics Teaching in the Middle School*, 2(4), 230–236.

van Reeuwijk, M. and M. R. Meyer. (Spring 2004). "Dot Patterns and Number Strips: Investigating Regularity With Applets," *On Math*, National Council of Teachers of Mathematics, Reston, VA.

Webb, D.C., T. Dekker, J. de Lange, and M. Abels. (2004). "Classroom assessment as a basis for teacher change" In T. A. Romberg (Ed.) *Standards-Based Mathematics Assessment in Middle School*. Teachers College Press, Columbia University. NY, 223–235.

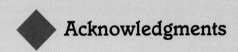

Acknowledgments for MiC Development 1991-1997

We at Encyclopædia Britannica Educational Corporation extend our thanks to all who had a part in making this program a success. Some of the participants instrumental in the program's development are as follows:

Allapattah Middle School
Miami, Florida
Nemtalla (Nikolai) Barakat

Ames Middle School
Ames, Iowa
Kathleen Coe
Judd Freeman
Gary W. Schnieder
Ronald H. Stromen
Lyn Terrill

Bellerive Elementary
Creve Coeur, Missouri
Judy Hetterscheidt
Donna Lohman
Gary Alan Nunn
Jakke Tchang

Brookline Public Schools
Brookline, Massachusetts
Rhonda K. Weinstein
Deborah Winkler

Cass Middle School
Milwaukee, Wisconsin
Tami Molenda
Kyle F. Witty

Central Middle School
Waukesha, Wisconsin
Nancy Reese

Craigmont Middle School
Memphis, Tennessee
Sharon G. Ritz
Mardest K. VanHooks

Crestwood Elementary
Madison, Wisconsin
Diane Hein
John Kalson

Culver City Middle School
Culver City, California
Marilyn Culbertson
Joel Evans
Joy Ellen Kitzmiller
Patricia R. O'Connor
Myrna Ann Perks, Ph.D.
David H. Sanchez
John Tobias
Kelley Wilcox

Cutler Ridge Middle School
Miami, Florida
Lorraine A. Valladares

Dodgeville Middle School
Dodgeville, Wisconsin
Jacqueline A. Kamps
Carol Wolf

Edwards Elementary
Ames, Iowa
Diana Schmidt

Fox Prairie Elementary
Stoughton, Wisconsin
Tony Hjelle

Grahamwood Elementary
Memphis, Tennessee
M. Lynn McGoff
Alberta Sullivan

Henry M. Flagler Elementary
Miami, Florida
Frances R. Harmon

Horning Middle School
Waukesha, Wisconsin
Connie J. Marose
Thomas F. Clark

Huegel Elementary
Madison, Wisconsin
Nancy Brill
Teri Hedges
Carol Murphy

Hutchison Middle School
Memphis, Tennessee
Maria M. Burke
Vicki Fisher
Nancy D. Robinson

Idlewild Elementary
Memphis, Tennessee
Linda Eller

Jefferson Elementary
Santa Ana, California
Lydia Romero-Cruz

Jefferson Middle School
Madison, Wisconsin
Jane A. Beebe
Catherine Buege
Linda Grimmer
John Grueneberg
Nancy Howard
Annette Porter
Stephen H. Sprague
Dan Takkunen
Michael J. Vena

Jesus Sanabria Cruz School
Yabucoa, Puerto Rico
Andreíta Santiago Serrano

John Muir Elementary School
Madison, Wisconsin
Julie D'Onofrio
Jane M. Allen-Jauch
Kent Wells

Kegonsa Elementary
Stoughton, Wisconsin
Mary Buchholz
Louisa Havlik
Joan Olsen
Dominic Weisse

Linwood Howe Elementary
Culver City, California
Sandra Checel
Ellen Thireos

Mitchell Elementary
Ames, Iowa
Henry Gray
Matt Ludwig

New School of Northern Virginia
Fairfax, Virginia
Denise Jones

Northwood Elementary
Ames, Iowa
Eleanor M. Thomas

Orchard Ridge Elementary
Madison, Wisconsin
Mary Paquette
Carrie Valentine

Parkway West Middle School
Chesterfield, Missouri
Elissa Aiken
Ann Brenner
Gail R. Smith

Ridgeway Elementary
Ridgeway, Wisconsin
Lois Powell
Florence M. Wasley

Roosevelt Elementary
Ames, Iowa
Linda A. Carver

Roosevelt Middle
Milwaukee, Wisconsin
Sandra Simmons

Ross Elementary
Creve Coeur, Missouri
Annette Isselhard
Sheldon B. Korklan
Victoria Linn
Kathy Stamer

St. Joseph's School
Dodgeville, Wisconsin
Rita Van Dyck
Sharon Wimer

St. Maarten Academy
St. Peters, St. Maarten, NA
Shareed Hussain

Sarah Scott Middle School
Milwaukee, Wisconsin
Kevin Haddon

Sawyer Elementary
Ames, Iowa
Karen Bush Hoiberg

Sennett Middle School
Madison, Wisconsin
Brenda Abitz
Lois Bell
Shawn M. Jacobs

Sholes Middle School
Milwaukee, Wisconsin
Chris Gardner
Ken Haddon

Stephens Elementary
Madison, Wisconsin
Katherine Hogan
Shirley M. Steinbach
Kathleen H. Vegter

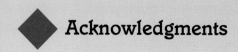

Acknowledgments

Stoughton Middle School
Stoughton, Wisconsin
Sally Bertelson
Polly Goepfert
Jacqueline M. Harris
Penny Vodak

Toki Middle School
Madison, Wisconsin
Gail J. Anderson
Vicky Grice
Mary M. Ihlenfeldt
Steve Jernegan
Jim Leidel
Theresa Loehr
Maryann Stephenson
Barbara Takkunen
Carol Welsch

Trowbridge Elementary
Milwaukee, Wisconsin
Jacqueline A. Nowak

W. R. Thomas Middle School
Miami, Florida
Michael Paloger

Wooddale Elementary Middle School
Memphis, Tennessee
Velma Quinn Hodges
Jacqueline Marie Hunt

Yahara Elementary
Stoughton, Wisconsin
Mary Bennett
Kevin Wright

Site Coordinators

Mary L. Delagardelle—Ames Community Schools, Ames, Iowa

Dr. Hector Hirigoyen—Miami, Florida

Audrey Jackson—Parkway School District, Chesterfield, Missouri

Jorge M. López—Puerto Rico

Susan Militello—Memphis, Tennessee

Carol Pudlin—Culver City, California

Reviewers and Consultants

Michael N. Bleicher
Professor of Mathematics
University of Wisconsin–Madison
Madison, WI

Diane J. Briars
Mathematics Specialist
Pittsburgh Public Schools
Pittsburgh, PA

Donald Chambers
Director of Dissemination
University of Wisconsin–Madison
Madison, WI

Don W. Collins
Assistant Professor of Mathematics Education
Western Kentucky University
Bowling Green, KY

Joan Elder
Mathematics Consultant
Los Angeles Unified School District
Los Angeles, CA

Elizabeth Fennema
Professor of Curriculum and Instruction
University of Wisconsin-Madison
Madison, WI

Nancy N. Gates
University of Memphis
Memphis, TN

Jane Donnelly Gawronski
Superintendent
Escondido Union High School
Escondido, CA

M. Elizabeth Graue
Assistant Professor of Curriculum and Instruction
University of Wisconsin–Madison
Madison, WI

Jodean E. Grunow
Consultant
Wisconsin Department of Public Instruction
Madison, WI

John G. Harvey
Professor of Mathematics and Curriculum & Instruction
University of Wisconsin–Madison
Madison, WI

Simon Hellerstein
Professor of Mathematics
University of Wisconsin–Madison
Madison, WI

Elaine J. Hutchinson
Senior Lecturer
University of Wisconsin–Stevens Point
Stevens Point, WI

Richard A. Johnson
Professor of Statistics
University of Wisconsin–Madison
Madison, WI

James J. Kaput
Professor of Mathematics
University of Massachusetts–Dartmouth
Dartmouth, MA

Richard Lehrer
Professor of Educational Psychology
University of Wisconsin–Madison
Madison, WI

Richard Lesh
Professor of Mathematics
University of Massachusetts–Dartmouth
Dartmouth, MA

Mary M. Lindquist
Callaway Professor of Mathematics Education
Columbus College
Columbus, GA

Baudilio (Bob) Mora
Coordinator of Mathematics & Instructional Technology
Carrollton-Farmers Branch Independent School District
Carrollton, TX

Paul Trafton
Professor of Mathematics
University of Northern Iowa
Cedar Falls, IA

Norman L. Webb
Research Scientist
University of Wisconsin–Madison
Madison, WI

Paul H. Williams
Professor of Plant Pathology
University of Wisconsin–Madison
Madison, WI

Linda Dager Wilson
Assistant Professor
University of Delaware
Newark, DE

Robert L. Wilson
Professor of Mathematics
University of Wisconsin–Madison
Madison, WI

Alignment to NCTM Standards

Level 1 units

NCTM Standard	Picturing Numbers	Models You Can Count On	Expressions and Formulas	Take a Chance	Fraction Times	Figuring All the Angles	Comparing Quantities	Reallotment	More or Less
Communication	X	X	X	X	X	X	X	X	X
Connections	X	X	X	X	X	X	X	X	X
Reasoning and Proof	X	X	X	X	X	X	X	X	X
Representations	X	X	X	X	X	X	X	X	X
Problem Solving	X	X	X	X	X	X	X	X	X
Number and Operations	X	X	X	X	X			X	X
Geometry			X			X		X	X
Measurement			X			X	X	X	
Algebra			X				X		
Data Analysis and Probability	X			X					

MiC was designed to align to the NCTM *Principles and Standards for School Mathematics*. Emphasis on number concepts (ratio, proportion and percent) and number models and their application in and connections to the other strands provide a sound foundation for students' mathematical learning. Progressive Formalization, one of the tenets of the MiC curriculum design, helps students develop concepts from informal to pre-formal to formal throughout the curriculum. Connections within and among strands assist students as they make sense of the mathematics and provide ample opportunity for practice and reflection.

Level 2 units

NCTM Standard	Facts and Factors	Dealing with Data	Made to Measure	Operations	Packages and Polygons	Ratios and Rates	Building Formulas	Triangles and Beyond	Second Chance
Communication	X	X	X	X	X	X	X	X	X
Connections	X	X	X	X	X	X	X	X	X
Reasoning and Proof	X	X	X	X	X	X	X	X	X
Representations	X	X	X	X	X	X	X	X	X
Problem Solving	X	X	X	X	X	X	X	X	X
Number and Operations	X	X		X		X	X	X	
Geometry	X	X	X		X			X	
Measurement			X		X	X	X	X	
Algebra				X			X	X	
Data Analysis and Probability		X							X

Building on the informal concepts from Level 1, Level 2 MiC emphasizes the pre-formal development of concepts within and among all strands. Integers, proportional reasoning, and algebraic formulas become the emphasis for Level 2. The connections of these topics within the geometry and data strands form the basis for formalizing and applying formulas in Level 3. The curriculum design supports student learning at a pre-formal level while allowing select students to progress to formalization as they become ready.

Alignment to NCTM Standards

Level 3 units

NCTM Standard	Revisiting Numbers	Ups and Downs	It's All the Same	Graphing Equations	Insights into Data	Patterns and Figures	Looking at an Angle	Great Predictions	Algebra Rules!
Communication	X	X	X	X	X	X	X	X	X
Connections	X	X	X	X	X	X	X	X	X
Reasoning and Proof	X	X	X	X	X	X	X	X	X
Representations	X	X	X	X	X	X	X	X	X
Problem Solving	X	X	X	X	X	X	X	X	X
Number and Operations	X		X			X		X	X
Geometry		X	X	X	X	X	X		X
Measurement		X	X		X		X		
Algebra		X		X		X			X
Data Analysis and Probability					X			X	

Continuing the progressive formalization from Levels 1 and 2, Level 3 MiC emphasizes the formalization of algebraic concepts as well as number algorithms and geometric applications. Connections within and among strands provide opportunities for students to build on prior knowledge and develop completely the higher order thinking skills necessary for high school mathematics.